The Magic Lift

Meeting the Rani

Savita Singh

Ukiyoto Publishing

All global publishing rights are held by

Ukiyoto Publishing

Published in 2024

Content Copyright © Savita Singh

ISBN 9789361722325

All rights reserved.

No part of this publication may be reproduced, transmitted, or stored in a retrieval system, in any form by any means, electronic, mechanical, photocopying, recording or otherwise, without the prior permission of the publisher.

The moral rights of the author have been asserted.

This is a work of fiction. Names, characters, businesses, places, events, locales, and incidents are either the products of the author's imagination or used in a fictitious manner. Any resemblance to actual persons, living or dead, or actual events is purely coincidental.

This book is sold subject to the condition that it shall not by way of trade or otherwise, be lent, resold, hired out or otherwise circulated, without the publisher's prior consent, in any form of binding or cover other than that in which it is published.

www.ukiyoto.com

To the Rani of Jhansi, one of the bravest daughters of Bharat and my ideal

Contents

An Introduction to the Characters	1
Chapter 1	4
Chapter 2	9
Chapter 3	16
Chapter 4	20
Chapter 5	28
Chapter 6	32
Chapter 7	39
Chapter 8	44
Chapter 9	48
Chapter 10	51
Chapter 11	57
Chapter 12	62
Chapter 13	69
Chapter 14	74
Chapter 15	80
Chapter 16	89
Chapter 17	101
Chapter 18	106
Chapter 19	112
Chapter 20	117
Chapter 21	122
Chapter 22	126
Chapter 23	130
Chapter 24	133
Chapter 25	137
Chapter 26	145
Chapter 27	148
Chapter 28	153
Chapter 29	156
Chapter 30	165
Chapter 31	169
Chapter 32	174

Chapter 33	182
Chapter 34	187
Chapter 35	191
Chapter 36	195
Chapter 37	204
GLOSSARY	206
Author's Note	212
About the Author	*216*

An Introduction to the Characters

In the Present Day

The Rais

Radhika Rai: the main protagonist of this book

Brigadier Balwant Rai: Radhika's father

Neeru Rai (the junior Mrs. Rai): Radhika's mother

Karan Rai: Radhika's younger brother

Daadi Maa (the senior Mrs. Rai): Radhika's paternal grandmother

The Bhandaris

Sunny Bhandari: Radhika's classmate and friend

Bhanumati Bhandari (Mrs. Bhandari or Bhanu): Sunny's grandmother and Daadi Maa's neighbour

The cousins in Jhansi

Surendra: The son of Daadi Maa's cousin

Alok: Surendra's son

Niti: Surendra's daughter

Others

Dr. Dastoor: The head of the Department of History at the Delhi University

Dr. Shalini Mehta: A historian-cum-archaeologist from Stanford University, California, and currently a member of the Archaeological Survey of India

Shah Nawaz Khan (Khan to his friends): A helpful taxi driver

Back in 1857

Damodar Rao (yuvraj): Rani Laxmi Bai's adopted son

Ganga: The daughter that Radhika's ancestor Mukund Rai gave in service to Rani Laxmi Bai

Jhalkari: A member of Rani Laxmi Bai's all-women army and her duplicate

Kashi Bai: One of the three closest friends of Rani Laxmi Bai who performed important duties in the rani's forces and played an important role in the Revolt of 1857

Moropant: Rani Laxmi Bai's father

Mukund Rai: Radhika's ancestor

Munder: One of the three closest friends of Rani Laxmi Bai who performed important duties in the rani's forces and played an important role in the Revolt of 1857

Nana Saheb: The older son of the ruler of Bithoor

Rao Dulhaju: One of the Rani of Jhansi's top lieutenants, the one who ultimately betrayed her

Rao Saheb: The younger son of the ruler of Bithoor

Raja Gangadhar Rao: Rani Laxmi Bai's husband

Sunder: One of the three closest friends of Rani Laxmi Bai who performed important duties in the rani's forces and played an important role in the Revolt of 1857

Tatya Tope: The man who was Rani Laxmi Bai's guru and taught her how to handle arms

Chapter 1

It was a lovely morning for a ride, bright, sunny, cool, with a gentle breeze blowing. Radhika Rai, slim, about five feet four, fair of face and with sharp features that were blessed with beautiful large eyes, enjoyed riding at the riding school grounds in Rajouri, in J&K. She, along with her younger brother, Karan, five feet two, chubby, with his puppy fat yet to be shed, lovingly referred to by her as brat, finished their two hours there and returned to the Flag Staff House of the brigade, ravenous. Their father, Brigadier Balwant Rai, who was commanding the artillery brigade at Rajouri, was sitting at the head of the table, hidden behind a two-day-old paper. Rajouri being rather out of the way, they got newspapers late there. His wife, Mrs. Neeru Rai, still in a kaftan, was sipping a cup of tea. There was *poori chhole* for brunch. Generally referred to as Mrs. Rai junior, to distinguish her from Mrs. Rai senior, or Daadi Maa, Neeru served both Radhika and Karan. The two youngsters had hardly fallen upon the food when Brigadier Rai suddenly put down his paper and, looking at all of them, dropped the bombshell.

'By the way, orders have been issued. All families have to leave Rajouri and shift either into separated family at Jammu or go back home. Rajouri is being converted from a soft field to a hard field and that unfortunately means that families will no longer be allowed here,' he announced. Both Radhika and Karan looked at him, confused. But worse was to come.

Radhika had just finished her twelfth from the Kendriya Vidyalaya, or Central School, at Rajouri, and had been looking forward to going off to the hostel in Delhi University's Hindu College, where she had applied for history honours. Brigadier Rai had another year at Rajouri, and Karan was now going into the ninth standard and would continue to stay put with the parents. Brigadier Rai looked at his wife, Neeru, and continued.

'After a discussion, your mother and I have decided that instead of you all moving into separated family, she will shift with both you and Karan to Noida. As you know, your Daadi Maa has been living alone since your Daada passed away. We talked to her yesterday evening. She is delighted with the decision. Karan can attend Delhi Public School, which is right next door, and you, Radhika, can attend your college without having to live in a hostel.'

Both Radhika and Karan looked totally taken aback. For a few minutes, they could not take in what he was saying. Then it hit them. Radhika realised that all her dreams of independence and enjoyment had just turned into dust. She felt so indignant. She had been so looking forward to leaving home for the first time and living independently.

'Come on, Papa! Daadi Maa lives on the top floor of her block of apartments, and there is not even a lift to her flat,' Karan complained.

'Don't worry,' declared Brigadier Rai. 'I have already sent one of my most trusted men, who has run around and got official permission from Noida Authority. A lift is being installed there for the exclusive use of your Daadi Maa.' And he went back behind his paper, leaving both Radhika and Karan glaring at him. They both looked at each other angrily. According to them, it was the most unfair, unilateral decision taken by the parents. How could they do this to them! Both of them were fuming but knew there was no point in arguing. Once Brigadier Rai had made up his mind, he would not budge. After all, he was a *fauji*.

The brother and sister looked at their mother for support, but she was suddenly very busy with her breakfast. Radhika felt like throwing a tantrum, rolling on the floor, stamping her feet and declaring that she would not comply with the autocratic decision, but she did nothing of the sort. Instead, she left her breakfast half eaten and walked off to her room. As she was leaving the room, Brigadier Rai came out from behind his paper to tell her, 'Sort out what you would like to take to Daadi Maa's with you, will you? You all will be going to Delhi by the end of the week.'

Radhika didn't even bother to turn and look at him. Of all the mean things they had done to the two of them, she thought crossly, this was one of the worst. They had just pulled the rug from under their feet without so much as a by-your-leave.

In disgust, Radhika kept muttering under her breath, 'How could they do it? How could they?' But they had.

Radhika had no recollection of how she spent the rest of that day. Both Karan and she were feeling betrayed. Their mother tried her level best to cajole both of them by getting the cook to make their favourite foods for lunch and dinner, but everything tasted like sawdust in their mouths. All the brother and sister felt like telling her was that she too had stabbed them in the back. Both were most unhappy. Soon, Karan disappeared into his room and Radhika was left alone to fume.

She spent the day wondering how she would manage at Daadi Maa's place. She had had very limited interaction with her. Like most Indian women of the older generation, Daadi Maa had always favoured Karan, however brattish his behaviour, just because he was a boy. She was one of those who believed that girls should serve the boys in the family and Karan, the brat, invariably took advantage of this screwed up thought process of Daadi Maa's. And now they would be staying with her for all of her college years. What a shame! Daadi Maa was sure to expect her to go to college and return immediately after her classes were over. There would be no chance of hanging out with friends or enjoying any sort of freedom. Things would be as bad as if not worse than they had been in school. The only concession would be that she, Radhika, would not have to wear a uniform.

Even Karan was not too happy as, although he was Daadi Maa's favourite, he would miss his friends and especially the buddies who were attached to Brigadier Rai's establishment and with whom he had made friends. They all loved to pamper him as he hung out with them whenever he could. At Daadi Maa's, there was only her sour old cook Raghubir Singh, who was not too good, and a part-time cleaning woman who came daily. Here, in Rajouri, they were used to a wide variety of cuisines where food was concerned. At Daadi Maa's, there would be no fancy English food, or even pizzas or pasta. Daadi Maa believed in wholesome Indian food with plenty of vegetables and a meat dish twice a week as a concession to the children whenever they visited her.

'Damn it! Damn it! Why couldn't Mom stay with Papa or take up separated family at Jammu!' muttered Radhika, as she looked around her room.

There would definitely not be enough place at Daadi Maa's for all her things. She would have to either discard quite a few things or put them in storage with the other bits of luggage belonging to Papa and Mama.

For a long time, Radhika sat. She just did not feel like doing anything. Lunch was once again a silent affair with both the children, who looked sullen and grim. Mrs. Rai tried to cheer them up. After all, she would also be going with them. But for her it, would be a different ball game. She would be busy looking after Daadi Maa, who was rather demanding. Karan and Radhika were both going to be bored stiff. But all their glowering had no effect upon their father, who just ate his lunch as usual and went back to his office. Mrs. Rai tried to pacify Radhika, but she shook off her gentle hand and flounced off to her room. Karan had already come to terms with the new plan. At least now there was a lift at Daadi Maa's, and they would not have to climb the four flights of stairs to the four-bedroom-and-study penthouse occupied by their Daadi Maa.

'Thank you, God, for small mercies,' thought Radhika sarcastically and rolled her eyes when her mother pointed this out to her for the fourth or fifth time that day.

Chapter 2

It was ten days later. The brother and sister had finally settled in Noida as best as they could. Brigadier Rai had returned to Rajouri, leaving Radhika and Karan behind with Neeru, the junior Mrs. Rai. The children were still feeling let down but by now were resigned. They had no other option. Of course, their Daadi Maa, the senior Mrs. Rai, had been delighted when she had heard the news that for the next few years, she would be having the three living with her. Life for her had been rather lonely ever since her husband had passed away, as her only child, Balwant, had already joined the army and his family stayed with him at the various stations he was posted to. She did go over to visit them from time to time, and they also came over for most of the holidays, but it would be different when they would be staying the whole time. She really was delighted. Her penthouse had three bedrooms, along with a study, a living room, a kitchen, and an attached servants' quarter at the back. Each of the bedrooms had a small balcony attached to it. Mrs. Rai senior herself occupied the master bedroom, which had an en-suite bathroom. Mrs. Rai junior had been allotted the next big one, again with an en-suite bathroom, while Radhika got the smallest one, known as the guest room. The tiny study had been converted into a bedroom exclusively for Karan. He would have to share third bathroom, the one that was next to Radhika's room and also opened into the living room. The study was across the living room from the other three rooms.

The Magic Lift

As Brigadier Rai had promised, the lift, a state-of-the-art contraption, had already been installed. As the balcony of the small room that had been given to Radhika was the only one which looked out straight into a small courtyard at the back of the block of flats, the lift had been attached to the wall leading down from one side of it. It was a welcome addition as it made it very convenient for the entire family. They did not have to climb up the fifty-six steps of the stairwell. It was also their very own private lift. As the occupants of the flats below Daadi's were all either young or middle-aged, they had thought they could do without one and had not wanted to share in the expenditure of the installation of one. So, it belonged to the Rai family, for their exclusive use. The only drawback was that whoever used the lift had to pass through the small room coming or going and it was bound to interfere with the privacy of the person occupying it. But once again, there were no options.

Radhika started settling down and found Noida not all that bad. After Brigadier Rai had left the very first evening, she was leaning on her balcony, feeling bored, when she heard what seemed like a lot of shouting coming from the little park adjacent to their block of flats. She looked over to find what looked like a young man running karate classes. The class had both girls and boys in it. Radhika had done a course in self-defence in school. She decided that it would not be a bad idea if she joined these classes here too. It would be something to look forward to. Some of the boys in the class looked interesting, and she found her heart beating a tad faster than usual. Maybe . . . you never know, she thought. She decided that she must try and persuade Karan to join with her. That would legitimise her joining up. No one could then say that she had joined the classes because she had liked the looks of the boys attending the class. She found Karan lounging upon the comfortable drawing room sofa reading a comic. When she broached the subject to him, the brat refused outright.

'Come on. I am sure you will love it,' declared Radhika.

Karan looked at her shrewdly.

'You want to join because there are boys in the class,' he declared, smirking.

Radhika glared at him. 'Certainly not!' she put up her nose and sauntered out of the room, wishing she had boxed that smirk off the brat's face. 'The cheek of him. Me join because there are boys in the class? What a preposterous idea!' thought the indignant girl. 'Well, I will go it alone. It is high time I sailed out on my own. After all, I am now nearly seventeen. So what if till now, I have had no boyfriend!'

The very next day, Radhika ventured down to the park and joined the classes. As the instructor put the group through their paces, to her chagrin, Radhika found that there was a gaggle of giggling girls, all simpering and batting their eyes at the boys, and the instructor frowned upon them whenever he caught them doing that.

The karate class, which was held five days in a week, turned out to be quite good. It was a week later. Radhika returned from her class to find the brat sprawling on the sofa in Daadi Maa's living room, watching a match on the one TV that the house boasted. Ugh! Matches were so boring. She just didn't understand what boys found so interesting in them. Give her a good historical drama, like *Siyasat*, or a war movie any day, thought the girl. At present, she was seeing the serial *Jhansi ki Rani*. She marched up to her brother and snatched the remote from him.

'Don't you have to give your entrance exam for Delhi Public School tomorrow?' she demanded belligerently.

'Hey! Give back the remote to me! I have finished all my studies for tomorrow,' exclaimed Karan and leaped up to snatch back the remote. Radhika promptly jumped up on the sofa and held it above her head. 'You have seen enough for today,' she chanted. 'Anyway, cricket matches are boring.'

'No, they aren't! It is between Zimbabwe and England! Give me back the remote!' yelled Karan and lunged at her. He hit her so hard that Radhika fell off from the sofa. Now, Daadi Maa's living room, which actually seemed to be a throwback to a previous century, held many small occasional tables with porcelain figures arranged upon them. Lacy antimacassar covers graced the armrests and backs of the sofa and chairs. Also, there were glass cupboards full of priceless crockery that was seldom used.

As Radhika fell off the sofa, her right foot got entangled in one of the antimacassar covers on the armrest of the sofa and as it was swept off, it took with it all the things arranged upon the occasional table kept next to it. There was a crash and the sound of shattering porcelain.

Radhika landed upon the ground with a jarring thud and lay there completely winded. Karan landed beside her.

Even as the two of them wrestled for the remote, they heard the sound of Daadi Maa's stick as she walked rapidly towards the living room. They didn't hear Mrs. Rai junior, but she reached first. Then, with Daadi Maa beside her, both women stood looking into the living room, grim expressions upon their faces.

'What is happening here?' finally, Neeru, Mrs. Rai junior, demanded in a strangled voice.

'And why are you both fighting like hooligans on the floor?' demanded Daadi Maa, looking sternly at the brother and sister.

Radhika finally managed to roll over. Hiding the remote below her, she lifted her head and opened her mouth to say something but one look at all the destruction all around and she only managed a squeak. She knew how much her Daadi Maa prized all the ornaments in her living room, and they had broken not one, not two, but quite a few in one go.

Karan recovered first and complained, 'Daadi Maa, *didi* will not let me see my match.'

'But, Mom, doesn't he have to study as he has to give his entrance test for DPS tomorrow?' said Radhika, turning over and giving her brother a box.

'Ouch! That's unfair!' wailed Karan. 'I have finished studying.'

'How well you have studied we'll know only tomorrow. Now, get up both of you. I am ashamed of you. Fighting like street urchins. Have you no manners?' scolded Neeru.

Both the children scrambled up quickly and stood looking equally guilty.

'I want to see my match, Mom,' declared Karan mutinously.

'You have been seeing it all evening. Now, it is my turn. I want to see *Jhansi ki Rani*,' declared Radhika vehemently, glaring at him and clinging on to the remote.

Suddenly, she found someone had firmly taken the remote from her and switched off the TV.

'You can both go to your rooms. No more TV today for either of you,' said Neeru, looking angry.

'Daadi Maa, please,' wheedled Karan, looking at his grandmother pleadingly.

Radhika could see the expression on Daadi Maa's face softening up. Really, if she allowed the brat to see the TV after what had gone by, it would be most unfair. But Daadi Maa was too shrewd for that. She addressed both of them.

'Apologise to your Mom, both of you. And after that, young lady, you come to my room. I want to show you something interesting.'

'Interesting? In what way?' asked Radhika, pursing her lips. She was suspicious. It was bound to be something boring.

'You are interested in the Rani of Jhansi,' said Daadi Maa, 'right?'

'Yes, Daadi Maa,' said Radhika. 'She is my favourite historical character.'

'Then, come along.' And turning, Daadi Maa walked back to her room.

'What about me?' asked Karan with a woebegone face. 'I am sorry, Ma. I really am sorry,' said he, holding his ears. Radhika felt bad for him. He was not really a bad sort, even if he annoyed her sometimes. But already, Neeru had melted. 'Well, first of all, you can clean up the living room and then I suppose you can watch your match, but only till dinner.'

The brat meekly set about cleaning the living room. He did not even protest that Radhika should share his punishment, as he had, after all, got his way. Radhika didn't have the heart to start another shindig. So, she left the room and went along to Daadi Maa's room, wondering what her grandmother wanted to show her.

Chapter 3

Daadi Maa's room was the master bedroom of the penthouse. Not only was it larger than the rest but it overlooked the garden next door. It held a Godrej cupboard with a locker in it for any valuables, a chest of drawers, a beautiful old-fashioned antique dressing table with a full-length mirror, and a little study table with a comfortable study chair. Above this, upon a glass shelf sat silver, gold, and marble idols of many gods of the Indian pantheon in her *mandir*. Every morning, after her bath, Daadi Maa sat in the chair, as she found it difficult to sit upon the floor, and read from the Bhagavad Gita, the Ramayan, or some other religious book for at least an hour before breakfast. And, at that time, woe betide anyone creating any kind of disturbance in the house. Everyone had to tiptoe around, and the children found it irksome as no breakfast would be served before Daadi Maa had finished her prayers. Karan was invariably caught making a racket of some sort and always declared that he had had no idea that Daadi Maa was at her prayers. So, now Daadi Maa had taken to announcing the beginning and the end of her prayer hour by ringing a silver bell that she kept in the *mandir*.

'Sit,' said Daadi Maa, pointing at the chair to Radhika as she retrieved a bunch of keys from her dressing table drawer and opened her Godrej cupboard. Radhika had never had a peek inside it and was interested in having a look. To her disappointment, all she saw was a stack of expensive-looking *sarees* and what looked like odds and ends stuffed inside. She wondered what was so precious about what looked like junk to her for it to be kept so carefully inside a Godrej cupboard. She soon found out.

Daadi Maa stood upon her toes and pulled out what looked like an old, battered tin box from the upper shelf. She brought it to the study table and placed it there. To Radhika's surprise, it had a very old-fashioned kind of lock on it. Daadi Maa picked out a small, equally old-fashioned key from the bunch she had taken from the dressing table drawer and opened the lock. Taking off the lock, she threw open the lid of the box. Radhika leaned towards it, eager to see what it contained. To her utter disappointment, all it contained was a thick notebook and a much-used leather-bound ledger of sorts.

'Do you know what this is, my dear?' Daadi Maa asked her, as she reverently lifted first the notebook and then the ledger out of the battered tin box.

'It looks like one of those ledgers that our *bania* uses in his shop,' said Radhika, sounding disappointed.

'Not really. This happens to be a ledger in which your ancestor, Mukund Rai, who took part in the Uprising of 1857, fighting from the side of the Rani of Jhansi, wrote his day-to-day account of the events happening then.'

Radhika got a jolt and nearly fell off her chair. 'Really, Daadi Maa! I never knew this!' she exclaimed. 'May I read it?' she asked excitedly, stretching her hands towards the ledger.

Daadi Maa laughed hearing the excitement in her voice. 'You may, but you cannot,' she said mysteriously.

'What do you mean by that?' asked Radhika, frowning. Really, sometimes, the old lady could be as exasperating as Karan.

'Because it is mostly in Awadhi and Hindi,' said Daadi Maa, smiling.

Disappointment engulfed Radhika. Hindi she could have read, but Awadhi, although the script would be Devnagri, the language would be totally different. She was still scowling when Daadi Maa dropped the notebook that she had picked up from on top of the ledger into her lap.

'But you can read the English translation of it, which I got a scholar to do a few years back.'

'Ooh!' was all Radhika could say as she caught it.

'Take it to your room and be careful with it,' admonished Daadi Maa softly.

Radhika could not believe her ears. She picked up the notebook and got up to go. On an impulse, she hugged Daadi Maa. She was sure going to have a ball of a time reading history being made, directly from the pen of one of her ancestors. What a lovely thing to look forward to for the next few weeks!

As Radhika was leaving the room, she heard Daadi Maa say distinctly, 'And don't let my favourite get his hands upon it. I don't think he is ready for it yet.'

Radhika turned around and glimpsed a twinkle in the old lady's eyes. It warmed the cockles of her heart like a hug. Daadi Maa was not a bad sort. She loved her granddaughter in her own way. Radhika smiled at her and sailed off to her room, the notebook clutched to her chest. She was smiling and feeling much better by this time. She would read it whenever she got the time, but first, she had to sort out what she would wear the next morning, as the next day would be her very first day at the university and she was a little apprehensive about it. She had heard much about the ragging that went on there.

Chapter 4

It was nearly ten o'clock when the autorickshaw drew to a halt in front of the gate of Hindu College. Radhika peeped out from inside it, and her heart sank. She could see that a whole lot of students were milling around at the entrance. It was obvious that groups of seniors were roaming around and catching the fucchas, as the freshers were called, and ragging them. She spotted some youngsters doing *utthak baithak* while pulling each other's ears. Even girls were not being left alone. A group of girls was making two girls sing and dance. Another mixed group was standing, waiting for its next victim as the first five victims sat upon the ground, looking miserable.

Radhika had half a mind to turn tail and go back home. But she had already stepped down, and before she could scramble back into the auto, the mixed group was upon her.

'Here comes our latest heroin!' laughed one girl.

'Come on. Catch her before she vanishes. We have found the ideal bride for our groom here,' said another.

'Come on, fuccha! How would you like to get married today?' demanded another voice.

'Excuse me?' said Radhika desperately, but already she had been surrounded. She just managed to pay the auto driver before she was herded inside the college. She found another newcomer, a fat, pimply boy, pushed towards her.

'Come on, how about escorting your bride up the aisle,' shouted someone.

'Hey! You can't do this to me!' protested Radhika.

'The bride doesn't like the groom, friends. What about changing him?' chortled a girl. The whole group roared with laughter.

'I think she would prefer to marry that tree there,' said another girl, pointing to a huge tree mischievously.

Immediately, the would-be groom was pushed aside and handed a drum.

'Beat this for the *baraat*,' he was instructed. The poor chap started beating it as loudly as he could.

The ring leader of the group was a tall, handsome boy with sharp features, a cheeky grin, and deep dimples in his cheeks.

'Hey, Sunny, you lead the bride to the tree. Tie her *dupatta* to it,' suggested someone.

'But she is wearing jeans,' protested Sunny. 'Malini, lend her yours. Tut! Tut! A bride without her modesty. What is the world coming to?' said Sunny, mimicking a famous mother-in-law of the silver screen.

The next moment, someone had draped a *dupatta* over Radhika's head and she was being led towards the tree famously known as the Virgin tree. There, with another newcomer forced to act as a priest, Radhika was solemnly made to take seven rounds of the tree and declared married to it while the entire group roared with laughter. Poor Radhika just went red in the face. She looked daggers at their leader, Sunny, who was smiling the broadest, and felt like smacking him. But then she decided to be a sport and joined in the laughter, even going up to the tree and kissing it. That took the raggers by surprise and they clapped loudly and cheered. The girl who had lent her *dupatta* recovered it from Radhika and smiled at her.

'Good for you,' she said under her breath. Their leader, Sunny, had already turned away. He called over his shoulder, 'Now, leave the new bride with her new husband for their honeymoon, Malu.' And he grinned at Radhika.

Radhika could have hit him with pleasure but decided that it was better to be prudent and get inside the college building before some other group caught her and ragged her.

The whole day went off in a haze. At the end of the classes that day, in the afternoon, Radhika sat in the bus for Noida, thankful to have found a window seat. But she was not too happy when she saw Sunny, the leader of the raggers who had ragged her that morning, also getting into it. He grinned upon seeing her.

'So, how was the honeymoon?' he asked flippantly, plonking himself down next to her.

Radhika glared at him, not deigning to reply. She looked around for another empty seat, but the bus was already full to capacity and many boys and girls were standing. She had half a mind to get up and stand but was too tired. All she could do was turn her head and look out of the window determinedly.

At last, the bus started. Everyone seemed to be chattering at the same time. Some of the seniors were still ragging the juniors. Thankfully, no one approached Radhika. Maybe it had something to do with Sunny sitting next to her. He seemed to be quite popular. Quite a few students came up to him to talk to him and give Radhika the once over. It was most irritating. Radhika just kept her face turned towards the window. She felt like declaring, 'Look, I am not with this joker.'

Just then, the bus came to a halt at Kashmiri Gate. Radhika looked out of the window, at the hustle and bustle outside. Their driver went off to buy some *beedis* for himself. Suddenly, there was a big commotion near the bus. Radhika saw one of the boys who had got off the bus trying to scramble back into the bus. But four or five typical *gunda*-type boys had surrounded him and their leader, in the best tradition of the Indian cinema villains, had unbuckled his belt and had now started raining blows upon the boy, yelling all the time, '*Sala. Mera naam Lacchu hai. Jaanta hai!*' (Fool. My name is Lacchu. Do you know that!)

Around her, there was complete stunned silence in the bus.

Radhika gasped. 'What is he doing? Why is he bashing up that poor boy?'

'Shut up!' ordered Sunny, 'and keep sitting.' He was looking equally shocked, but Radhika had already squeezed her way out of the seat past Sunny. She dashed to the front of the bus and jumped down. The boy who was being bashed up kept falling down, but the bully just propped him back up against the bus and now, besides the bully with the belt, the other bullies had joined in with their fists and boots. A group of spectators had gathered, but no one was making a move to stop them. By now, the victim was bleeding badly from his nose and one of his eyes was bruised shut.

Radhika saw red. Without a thought that she might get hurt, she just barged into the circle of bullies, caught hold of the victim and, dragging him out, pushed him back into the bus. The four bullies, taken by surprise, just gaped. By this time, others had been galvanised into action also. Willing hands pulled Radhika back into the bus. The bullies recovered and tried to follow her into the bus but found Sunny and two other boys blocking their way. As they were standing above the bullies, they had the advantage. Even as they shoved the bullies away, the driver of the bus, who had by now returned from his short break, started the bus and they shot away.

Inside the bus, there was utter chaos. The youngster who had been beaten up was bleeding badly. One girl lent her *dupatta*, and they tore it up and used it as bandages. Another offered him water, and someone else forced a chocolate upon him. Ten minutes later, the boy's bus stop came and fortunately, there was no one there. The boy, who had recovered a little by now, insisted that his home was nearby and that he would be able to make it on his own. Two of his friends from the bus volunteered to go with him and see him safely home.

Once they all were back in their seats, Sunny turned to Radhika. 'That was very foolish of you. You could have got injured. Those boys were not normal students but *gundas*.'

Radhika swallowed and tried to reply flippantly but found she had lost her voice. She opened her mouth to retort but no sound came out. She found she was shivering. Suddenly, she found Sunny's arm around her and he was patting her gently.

'It is ok. It is ok. You were very brave. Now don't go and faint on me,'

Immediately, Radhika flared up. 'Excuse me! I am not one of those kinds of girls,' she exclaimed indignantly, suddenly finding her voice. She shook off his arm, sat up straight, and determinedly looked out of the window. How could she have forgotten that this was the boy who had also led a group of raggers in the morning. Of course, they had been more gentle, but still . . .

At Noida, when she got off at the bus stop in Sector 29, to her chagrin, she found Sunny also getting off there. This made her see red once again. Really, what did he think, that after what had happened, she was incapable of going home alone? Then, she decided that it was better to ignore him completely. Maybe if she did not give him any lift, he would go away.

As Radhika made her way back to the society where her grandmother lived, her temper rose as she saw that Sunny was still following her. She reached the gate of the society and then decided to catch the bull by the horn. Turning around and putting her hands on her hips, she faced him belligerently.

'Why are you following me?' She demanded, glaring at him.

The boy looked surprised and then he grinned cheekily. 'I am not following you.'

'Then why have you come here? I'll call the *chaukidar*!' declared Radhika.

'Go ahead and do so,' challenged the boy and stood smiling insolently at her.

'*Chaukidar! Chaukidar!*' yelled Radhika, looking towards the gate of the society. The Gurkha who was usually on duty came running out to see who was yelling for him. He skidded to a halt when he spotted the two of them.

'*Kya hua, didi? Bhaiya, ye mujhe kyon bula rahin theen?*' (What happened, sister? Brother, why was she calling out to me?) he demanded of Sunny.

'*Tum isko jaantey ho?*' (You know him?) asked Radhika incredulously.

'*Ye Bhandari Memsahab key naati hain naa. Yaheen tou rahtey hain,*' (He is the grandson of Mrs. Bhandari and lives here only) informed the guard.

'I, unfortunately, happen to live in this building myself,' laughed Sunny.

'What? You live here?' asked Radhika, turning back to Sunny and literally gaping at him.

'Yes. My grandmother lives on the ground floor, below your grandmother. I know who you are,' he declared smugly.

Radhika pursed her lips angrily. 'You are Mrs. Bhandari's grandson?' she demanded, remembering that her grandmother and Mrs. Bhandari were the best of friends.

Actually, Mrs. Bhanumati Bhandari was the widow of late General Bhandari and her son-in-law was in the diplomatic service and posted to some African country. Hence, her grandson Sunny was staying with her for the duration of his bachelor's degree, while he prepared for joining the Civil Services like his father. Despite the fact that the two ladies were so close, the only reason Radhika had not met either her or Sunny till now was because the Bhandari family had been away, to their farm in Panchkula, for a while and had returned just a day or two earlier.

By now, Sunny was roaring with laughter. Radhika felt like clobbering him but suddenly saw the funny side of everything and found herself joining in the laughter.

'Let us shake hands. Friends?' asked Sunny, extending his hand. Radhika hesitated a moment, then took the offered hand. The Gurkha guard was looking on bewildered and shaking his head. Giving him cheeky grins, both the teenagers entered their society and bidding goodbye to each other went their ways, Radhika to find her lift and Sunny to the flat occupied by his grandmother.

Chapter 5

Life at number 400, the penthouse of the set of flats named Indradhanush House, occupied by Mrs. Rai senior, or Daadi Maa, and now also by the rest of the Rai family, was slow. The children missed the parties that marked the celebration of every festival in army circles. Generally, kids were not allowed at any formal parties held in the messes. But most festivals are celebrated with gusto in the army clubs, and the children all enjoy themselves immensely there. Here, there was an army club, but Brigadier Rai had yet to get membership of it. So, they could not attend any functions held their on their own. They could only go if Daadi Maa went, as she was a member, and she went religiously every Saturday evening for the tambola session. Radhika and Karan found these gatherings rather boring. But ever since the Bhandaris had returned, things had perked up. Mrs. Bhandari was also an avid tambola player. The two old ladies invariably sat together with the junior Mrs. Rai. It was left to the children Sunny, Radhika, and Karan to fetch the snacks and drinks for the ladies. Sunny introduced Radhika to the well-stocked library of the club, from where she and Karan could borrow books and magazines on their grandmother's card.

Talking about books, Brigadier Rai had always regaled the children with tales of the oldest lending library in Delhi and of the Lalaji who had been the owner of this library when Brigadier Rai himself had been a child. He had cycled down to borrow comics and books from the shop, which at that time, had been located on Baba Khadak Singh Marg. It had shifted to its present location only much later. Lalaji had been a formidable old man with a huge paunch and only a twisted bit of hair, or *shikha*, upon the back of his shaved head. The library had been well stocked and very popular with all the teenagers of that time. Lalaji himself had been a gruff character and woe betide any child who returned one of the borrowed comics or books in a mutilated condition, Lalaji was not above boxing or twisting the ears of said child. Now, the library was located in Shankar Market and was run by Lalaji's daughter.

Brigadier Rai had done one good thing before he left for Rajouri. He had taken both Karan and Radhika over to Lalaji's library and introduced them to Lalaji's daughter. Now, they could take the bus or the Delhi Metro down once a month to CP and borrow a whole lot of books and comics for a whole month at a nominal cost from there also. It was the best thing Brigadier Rai had done. Karan had, of course, gone in for comics, while Radhika had taken Meg Cabots, Agatha Christies, and Barbara Cartlands. But, in spite of having four or five borrowed books to choose from now, Radhika found the journal written by their ancestor the most fascinating to read. After all, this dealt with the very own history of their family. Radhika showed it to Sunny, who wanted to go through it after she had finished with it.

Every evening after dinner, Radhika would retire to her room and bury myself in the English translation of the journal written by their ancestor Mukund Rai. But very soon, she realised that the English translation was not too good. It lacked the flavour that probably was there in the original. On the third day itself, she decided that she would try and read the journal in the original. So what if she knew only Hindi and little or no Awadhi. She could always ask Daadi Maa, who knew Awadhi quite well.

Radhika wanted to borrow the original manuscript, but Daadi Maa refused to part with the precious tome. She was afraid it would get torn. So, every day, after dinner, Radhika had an hour-long stint with Daadi Maa and the journal in Daadi Maa's room. Both of them read it slowly, but the colours of those times came out so sharply that it was fascinating to read. Then Radhika would go back to her room and continue with the English translation.

Her ancestor had written down the reaction of the people of Jhansi when fourteen-year-old Manikarnika, alias Manu, the daughter of Moropant and Bhagirathibai of Pune who had migrated to Kashi, was married to forty-year-old Raja Gangadhar Rao of Jhansi. There had been so much celebration as the Raja's first wife had passed away childless and now the people had hope of getting an heir from the new wife, who had been re-named Laxmi Bai.

Mukund Rai had written how he had given one of his three daughters, Ganga, who was of a similar age to the new queen, to serve the new queen as a maid-in-waiting. The girl would live in the palace with the new queen and remain unmarried. If she got married, she would have to leave the service of the queen.

The first time the girl had gone home for a bit of leave when her mother was ill, she had reported that the new queen had refused to treat these serving girls who came from good families as servants and insisted on treating them as companions and friends. She also insisted on teaching them wrestling, riding, sword fighting, etc. The queen had won the hearts of all of them, and they all were willing to do anything to please her.

Anyone reading the journal got a good idea about what kind of a person Laxmi Bai was. Not only had she been a tomboy, but she had also been fully into physical fitness and believed in discipline. She had obviously been brought up in a very free atmosphere, more like a boy than a girl of that time. Her childhood companions had always been boys. There was mention of Nana Saheb and Rao Saheb, the sons of the ruler of Bithoor, and Tatya Tope, the man who had been her *guru* and who had taught her how to handle arms. In fact, after her marriage to the Maharaja of Jhansi, her father, Moropant, had also been given a good post in Jhansi and settled down there to be near his only child.

Chapter 6

It was about a month later. Radhika stood in front of the notice board in the college, casually going over the announcements pinned to it when one caught her eye. A seminar was being held by the Historical Society of the university in collaboration with the Archaeological Survey of India. The topic of discussion would be the life and time of Rani Laxmi Bai, the Rani of Jhansi, and her contribution to the freedom struggle of 1857. A debate was going to be held between professor Dr. Dastoor, the head of the Department of History at Delhi University, and a Dr. Shalini Mehta, a historian-cum-archaeologist from Stanford University, California, who now worked for the Archaeological Survey of India. Anyone who wanted to attend was cordially invited to do so.

Radhika looked at the name of Dr. Shalini Mehta. It looked familiar. Then it struck her. Of course, it was Shalini *didi*. Shalini's father was General Mehta, now retired, who had been her father's first commanding officer and then later his brigade commander. Shalini had been a young woman of about twenty-five, and as they were all staying in a soft field area, whenever there was an official party and Shalini was home on holiday, she had been dumped with the responsibility of looking after all the younger kids. They all had had a blast of a time with her. She had been their favourite *didi*. She had been doing her doctorate at that time. Radhika immediately decided that she must attend the seminar. Maybe she could show the journal of her ancestor to Shalini *didi*. It would be exciting. She immediately caught hold of Sunny, who was not very keen but finally agreed half-heartedly.

The auditorium where the seminar was being held was a small one in the Arts Faculty. Once classes were over, Sunny and Radhika made their way over to it. To their surprise, they found it nearly full. They managed to find two seats at the back, but as the auditorium was small, the podium was visible.

To Radhika's surprise, Shalini *didi* turned out to be completely different from the girl Radhika remembered. She had become a middle-aged lady with her hair tied in a loose bun at the nape of her neck. She had on soda glasses and wore a simple cotton *saree*. She had a wide smile, with just a trace of lipstick on her lips.

Dr. Dastoor was tall and thin as a rake, with protruding eyes behind thick soda glasses, a bulbous nose, and loose lips, which Radhika thought made him unfortunately look rather like a toad.

Dr. Dastoor introduced Dr. Mehta as a visiting faculty who at the moment was engaged in the restoration of the old palace of the Rani of Jhansi, which had fallen into disrepair after the British had confiscated it once the rani had died fighting.

Finally, Dr. Mehta got up and adjusting the mike at the podium, smiled at the audience in front of her.

'Good afternoon, everyone. I am glad to see that there is so much interest in the Uprising of 1857, which the British labelled as a rebellion but which was actually our first war of independence. In that war, surprisingly, quite a few queens played a big part. Begum Hazrat Mahal and

Rani Laxmi Bai are two of the most well-known names. Today, I have been invited here to tell you something about Rani Laxmi Bai, the great Rani of Jhansi, who fought till her last breath and died fighting.

'We all have heard the story of how brave the rani was. Remember the famous poem by Mrs. Subhadra Kumari Chauhan '*Khoob Ladi Mardani, Woh Tou Jhansi Wali Rani Thi*'? We all have read it during our school days. Well, the rani of course believed a hundred percent in physical fitness, and it was a well-known fact that she considered that as warriors, women could be as good as men. She was an only child and had been brought up with boys like Nana Saheb and Rao Saheb in the Maratha court and so right from childhood, she had learnt how to fight with weapons. She was also fearless and considered herself a better rider than Nana and Rao.

'There is the story of how once she and Nana were out riding when Nana's horse was startled and threw off Nana. Nana would have been trampled if Manu, who later became Laxmi Bai, had not swept up and literally dragged him onto her horse and brought him back.

'In a time when women mainly observed *purdah*, Rani Laxmi Bai insisted that all her lady companions, whom she refused to treat as maids and instead treated as *sahelis*, or friends, also practice physical fitness. She taught them wrestling, sword fighting, shooting, *malkhamb*, etc.

'Besides being very conscious of physical fitness, the rani was very religious and also knew more than one language. She knew Marathi, which was her mother tongue, and learnt Bundelkhandi, and even knew English.

'When her husband died, it is said that she wrote to Queen Victoria herself to grant her adopted son Damodar Rao the right to become the next ruler of Jhansi.

'The rani was a very able administrator and a great strategist and she had planned for the defence of Jhansi so well that the siege of Jhansi would never have succeeded had she not been betrayed by one of her own men. The rani escaped by jumping with her horse from the ramparts of her fort, her son tied upon her back, and went to Kalpi, where Rao Saheb and others were camped.

'The rani was known to be ambidextrous where plying the sword was concerned. She could stand up in her saddle, hold the reins of her horse in her mouth, and ply two swords at the same time.'

When Dr. Mehta finally ended, there was a loud round of applause. Then there was a question-and-answer session. One young student stood up and asked, 'Excuse me, Dr. Mehta. You have said that the rani knew English and probably wrote to Queen Victoria herself for the recognition of her adopted son as the rightful heir to the throne of Jhansi. My question is, is there any record anywhere that the rani knew English?'

'Yes, are there any documents, any letters, etc., written by her personally in English?' asked Dr. Dastoor, suddenly jumping into the fray.

Shalini Mehta turned and looked in surprise at Dr. Dastoor, who was sitting on the podium behind her.

'As you all know, the British burnt down the extensive library of the Maharaja of Jhansi. I don't think any actual document written in English by the rani in her own hand exists now.'

'Then, ma'am, you should not make such a claim that you cannot substantiate,' said Dr. Dastoor sharply.

Dr. Mehta looked a little taken aback. Generally, colleagues, even if they had differences between themselves, did not attack each other in public and that too in front of students. Then she recovered and retorted, 'We are busy renovating the old palace of the rani in Jhansi. We just might come across some proof, you never know, sir.' Then, turning around, she thanked the audience for listening to her patiently and without waiting for any more questions or discussion, walked off the podium. She did not wait around in the auditorium for the mandatory tea and biscuits either but just kept walking until she had left the hall. It was obvious that she was very upset by the way her colleague had behaved. The seminar was over. Radhika never got the opportunity to even talk with her, leave alone show her anything. She felt really disappointed and let down.

∧∧∧∧∧∧∧∧∧∧∧

A few days later, Radhika returned from her karate class, quickly gulped down the hot tea and cucumber sandwiches her mother always kept ready for her (the karate classes made Radhika ravenous), and went to her room. She lay upon her bed to read the English translation of the journal that Daadi Maa had given her. Ever since the seminar, she had been finding the journal more and more interesting. She had only been disappointed that on the day of the seminar, she had been unable to speak about it to Shalini *didi* before Shalini *didi* had walked off in a huff.

The journal had become very absorbing, and very soon, she found herself lost in the narration of her ancestor, how he had been present at the marriage of Manikarnika, whose name, according to tradition, had been changed on the day she was married to Raja Gangadhar Rao of Jhansi and she had become Rani Laxmi Bai. He had described how in the presence of all the powerful *sardars* of Jhansi, before Gangadhar Rao and Laxmi Bai had taken the seven auspicious circles of the sacred fire, Laxmi Bai had noticed that the hands of the old priest, who had been tying the knot between the veil worn by her and the shawl worn by Gangadhar Rao, had been shaking badly. Immediately, in a loud voice, she had called out to him to tie the knot so tightly that it would not open. That comment had made everyone present burst into laughter. But Gangadhar Rao, known for his erratic decisions and explosive temper, had frowned, not amused at all at this cheeky comment. There had been whispers around that at last, Jhansi had got a queen who would wear the pants and not be subservient to anyone.

Radhika was getting more and more impressed by the character of the Rani of Jhansi as she read about her. In that era, when most women had stayed in *purdah*, the rani had been an unbelievable exception. Radhika wished she could have been there then. She would have loved to meet the rani in person.

Dinner came and went, but Radhika hardly noticed it. She was so engrossed in the journal that she never realised until her body became stiff that more than three hours had passed. At last, she stretched and decided she could do with a walk. It would relax her. So, she changed into a t-shirt and jogging pants, took her torch from her dressing table drawer, and putting on sneakers, stepped out onto the balcony and into the lift to go down. She wanted to take some fresh air in the tiny garden located next door.

Chapter 7

The tiny park was deserted at that time of the night. But it was well lighted by a full moon, which gave it an almost magical look. The grass looked most inviting. Kicking off her sneakers, Radhika let the cool grass caress the soles of her feet. It felt wonderful. After a few rounds, she sat down upon one of the benches and just breathed in the fresh air deeply while lost in contemplation about what she had managed to read in the journal that evening. She wished Sunny was there and they could discuss what she had read. She had half a mind to ring him up on his mobile and ask him to join her in the park. Then she looked at her wristwatch and saw that it was nearly midnight. It was rather late in the day for a rendezvous. Instead, she just plucked a piece of grass and sat idly, tearing it to pieces and letting her mind just wonder slowly, her thoughts in the past. She wondered what her ancestor had been really like. Had he been as brave as the rani? What had his daughter been like, the daughter he had given in service to the rani? According to Dr. Mehta, or Shalini *didi*, as Radhika tended to think of her, all the girls in the service of the rani had to remain celibate but they were treated like friends by the rani and not maids. They all had been loyal to her, and many had given their life for her.

Radhika's reverie was suddenly interrupted by an ominous rumble. She came back to the present with a jerk. The park had been plunged into darkness. She looked up to see black clouds racing across the sky, obscuring the light from the full moon.

'Oh, oh! I think I'd better go back in. It looks like it is about to rain,' she muttered to herself, getting up hastily and putting on her sneakers. She slipped out of the park and was rushing back towards the waiting lift when the rain started. Without warning, it started pouring. Radhika just managed to reach the lift and opening the door almost fell inside it. She had to struggle to pull the door of the lift shut as a very strong wind had risen and the rain had become almost like a waterfall. At last, she managed to close the door of the lift and pressed the button for the top. The lift started moving slowly. Already, flashes of lightning were splitting the sky. Radhika could feel the rush of adrenalin in her body. She was soaked, and the heckles had risen all over her body and were standing at attention. Radhika was one of those people who are not too fond of thunder and lightning. She felt frightened. She generally preferred to put a pillow over her head and hide under a duvet during a storm.

The lift had barely moved halfway up when there was an awful bang, more of an explosion than anything else, making Radhika yelp and nearly jump out of her skin. Immediately, all the streetlights, which till then had been visible, went off. The power in the lift also went off. The generator should have taken over automatically, but something must have been wrong with it, because the lift stopped abruptly and then slowly started descending.

'Oh my God! Oh my God!' was all Radhika could exclaim as she pushed her fingers into her ears and shut her eyes tight because more explosions were following the first one and rain was falling in sheets. She sat down on the floor of the lift, shaking.

By the time the lift came to a rest at the bottom, Radhika was whimpering with fright. There was a click. The door of the lift had opened automatically. But Radhika would have to stay inside it as it was raining so hard and the storm that was raging outside was freaking her out.

It was a minute or two before she realised that there was no longer any sound coming from outside the lift. No sound of the falling rain, or the raging storm, or the thunder and lightning. Radhika willed herself to open her eyes, which had been screwed up tightly. It was pitch dark outside. But definitely there was no sound coming from there. Was the storm over already? Radhika remembered her torch and, taking it out of her pocket, showed it outside. There was no open courtyard, the one where the lift was situated. In fact, she seemed to be in some sort of an enclosed space.

Cautiously, Radhika stepped out of the lift and found herself standing upon what looked like old bricks. She showed her torch around. The beam lighted up walls made out of uneven rocks.

Sudden panic engulfed her. Had the lift crashed into the basement of the block of flats? But there had been no crash of any kind. Radhika turned around to rush back into the lift but found to her horror that there was no lift there. The light of her torch fell upon what looked like a solid rock wall. Where had the lift vanished too?

She turned and flashed her torch as far as she could. She seemed to be in some kind of a passage, a tunnel of sorts.

Panic began to grip her once again. Since she had no other option, she started walking down the tunnel. 'Shoot! This is a weird nightmare,' thought she to herself. 'But like all nightmares, it should end eventually,' she told herself bracingly. At the moment, she seemed to be right in the middle of it and was helpless to do anything about it.

The passage seemed to go on and on and on for a long time. It was very dusty and smelt musty and damp. Radhika was beginning to wonder when her nightmare would end when suddenly she saw what looked like an opening in the right side of the wall, a window-like opening, with soft light coming through it. Walking up to it, she peeped through it. At first, she could see nothing. She was about to flash her torch through it when some instinct made her halt. By now, her eyes were used to the gloom and she found herself looking into what appeared to be a large chamber of some sort. There was a huge four-poster bed in the centre of it, draped with gauzy curtains bellowing in a gentle breeze. There were a few oil lamps lit in the chamber, and she could see ornate chairs and stools lying around. Even as she watched, she saw a shadow move towards the bed. The shadow stood next to the bed and raised one arm and she was horrified to see that the person clutched a knife. Someone was trying to murder whoever was sleeping in the bed!

All this registered in the split second before Radhika was galvanised into action.

'Oh no! You don't!' she yelled, jumping into the room and racing towards the shadow. She leapt at the shadow and brought the person down with a flying tackle. There was a grunt as they both crashed to the floor of the room. The next few minutes were a blur. Radhika found herself struggling with the would-be assailant. The man was strong, but Radhika's self-defence and karate training came handy. She knocked his hand up and then twisted it out. There was an ominous crack, and with a scream, the man dropped the knife he had been holding. Radhika made a grab for it. By now, the door of the chamber had crashed open and people were pouring in. There was a thin cry coming from the bed. It had been a child whom the man had been trying to kill.

Radhika was distracted by the people pouring into the room and the intruder got a chance to throw Radhika off him. Jumping up, he vanished through the opening through which Radhika had entered. Obviously, he had entered through that same opening also. Radhika also jumped up and was about to follow when two hefty bodies caught hold of her and pinned her down. Before she could react, someone had hit her on the head with something and she blacked out.

Chapter 8

Rain was falling on her face. Radhika had to get out of it. She tried to get up but found that she could not move. She seemed to be lying on a hard floor. Another spray fell on her face. She could hear a murmur of voices. Had she fainted? Then it all came back with a rush. Her eyes flew open, and she tried to jump up, but groaned as her head nearly split with pain. She also realised that not only were her hands tied up but there was a gag tied upon her mouth. She found herself looking up into four or five anxious female faces. One of them had been sprinkling water upon her face from a glass that she held. Radhika groaned.

The women chattered excitedly in Hindi.

'She has revived,' said one. 'Let us take her to Maharani Sahiba.'

Another one poked Radhika in her shoulder, making her wince with pain. Obviously, she had bruised herself badly when she had fallen. She only hoped that she had not broken any bone.

'Here is the knife with which she was planning to kill the yuvraj,' declared another, brandishing the knife that the would-be assassin had dropped. Radhika shook her head hard, wincing as her head protested in pain, and tried to mumble that the knife did not belong to her but to another man, who had run away. She could hear a child crying softly from the direction of the bed. Just then, there was another commotion, as the door of the chamber was flung open once again and a young woman hurtled into the room. There was utter fear upon her face. She raced to the bed and snatching up the crying child, hugged him tightly to her chest. Only once the child had been soothed that she turned to where all the other females were standing, surrounding poor Radhika, who was trussed up like a chicken.

'What happened, Ganga?' asked the newcomer in Hindi.

All the women around Radhika stood respectfully, while the one holding the glass of water stepped forward.

'Rani Sahiba, this woman in a man's attire was planning to stab the yuvraj ji. She was running away when we caught her.'

The girl addressed as Ganga stepped up and said, 'With due respect, Maharani Sahiba, that was not the case.'

'Then what was the case?' asked the woman addressed as Maharani Sahiba who was holding the child.

'I entered first and this girl here was fighting with the other person, who was trying to get at the knife. Then she looked at us as we all burst in, and the man threw her off and ran off. I raced after him but he had disappeared into that hole in the wall. By the time I turned back, these others had knocked this one out and trussed her up,' said Ganga.

Radhika struggled with her bonds, trying her level best to say that the girl Ganga was right, but all she managed were some inarticulate sounds. The woman addressed as Maharani Sahiba indicated for the gag to be removed. They removed it and forced Radhika to sit up. Radhika spluttered and at last managed to say,

'That girl is right. It was that other man. In fact, I tackled him and stopped him, but he managed to escape.'

Radhika looked up at the woman addressed as Maharani Sahiba. She wondered the rani of which kingdom this lady was. Tall, on the stouter side, the lady was dressed in white pyjamas and a white *kurta*, upon which she wore a pearl necklace. Her features were good, her hair was shoulder length, and she was looking down at Radhika with speculation in her eyes.

'Who are you, and why was that man trying to murder my son, the yuvraj?'

'How should I know? I don't know who he was. I was by chance in the passage behind when I saw him raising his knife and without thinking just jumped into the room and tackled him,' said Radhika.

The rani looked at the hole in the wall and asked, 'Where does this hole lead to?' Did anyone of you know it was there?'

'It was behind that tapestry,' indicated one of the female guards, pointing to a crumpled carpet-like thing that lay upon the ground where it had fallen. Obviously, the hole in the wall had been hidden by the tapestry hanging upon the wall and so had been hidden from view.

'It opens into a tunnel which probably goes outside the palace and ends somewhere in the town,' said another of the women.

'I know where it goes,' one of the guards suddenly exclaimed. 'One branch of it ends in the *pilkhana* and another ends somewhere outside the town. My father told me about it once when I was a child.'

Now, all of them once again started concentrating upon Radhika. 'Who are you, and from where have you come?' demanded the rani.

'Listen, this is bizarre. I am Radhika Rai, from Noida.'

'Ah, so you are a visitor to our city from outside. And where is this Noida? I have not heard of it?' commented the woman who had been addressed as the rani. She showed no recognition at the mention of Noida.

'It is next to Delhi,' said Radhika.

'Do they wear such odd clothes there?' asked the rani.

Radhika chose to ignore this remark, asking instead, 'And you are the rani of . . . ?'

All the women looked at her, stunned. At last, one of them said, 'You don't know? You are in the presence of Maharani Laxmi Bai of Jhansi.'

Radhika, dumbfounded, felt the entire chamber whirling around her. It couldn't be!

Chapter 9

When Radhika came to her senses sometime later, it was to find herself lying upon the bed. Once again, someone was sprinkling water upon her face and even the rani was bending over her.

'Are you alright?' asked the rani anxiously. All Radhika could do was nod dumbly. She tried to sit up, and one of the girls bending over her helped her sit up. She looked around in a bewildered way, but the scene did not change. She was still in the chamber that she had entered through the hole in the wall, lighted with oil lamps. There was no electric light visible.

The rani sat down on one of the ornate chairs, still clutching the small boy to her. He was all of seven or eight. He sat upon the rani's lap and stared at Radhika with huge eyes full of curiosity.

'Now tell me again. Who are you, and what are you doing in my son's sleeping chamber with a knife?' asked the rani.

'That knife is not mine, ma'am,' protested Radhika heatedly. 'It belongs to the man who ran away from here.'

The rani smiled at her. 'Don't call me, ma'am. That is used for only *firangi* ladies. You can call me Rani Sahiba, like the rest here. Now, go on.'

Radhika felt rather odd as she recounted the story of how she had, while walking down the corridor past the chamber, spotted the assassin about to murder the little boy sitting on the rani's lap, how she, Radhika, had tackled him, and how he had escaped.

'Get someone to seal the opening and change the yuvraj's chamber forthwith,' ordered the rani.

Fortunately, no one asked Radhika what she had been doing in the tunnel or how she had landed up in it. They somehow assumed that as a visitor to the town, she had got into it from somewhere in the town below. She also realised that if she told them how, in actuality, she had gone out for a walk and because of a freak storm, her lift had thrown her not only into the tunnel but also more than a hundred years back in time, they would never believe her. They would think she was crazy.

'What do you do?' asked the rani.

'I am a student, Rani Sahiba. I am studying English honours.'

'What do you mean by English honours?' asked the rani, looking puzzled.

'It means my main subject is English,' explained Radhika.

The rani brightened up at hearing this. 'That is great. The lady from whom I was learning English has recently gone back to England. If you don't mind, you can help me progress with my learning the language.'

Radhika looked at her, wondering how to reply to this request. She would have liked to go back to her time and Noida, but her lift had vanished. She seemed to be stuck here in both time and place. She would have to bide her time until she could find her lift once again and go back. So, she nodded. The rani smiled once again.

'So, it is decided. Ganga, you take Radhika here under your wings. She will give me lessons in English every day. She will live with you all from today,' ordered the queen and dismissed everyone. As everyone started going out of the chamber, the girl addressed as Ganga caught hold of Radhika's arm and led her out too. Radhika followed her, too bemused at the turn events had taken. So, this was the daughter her ancestor had given as a *saheli* to the rani. Ganga would be her fourth- or fifth-great-grand-aunt, Radhika thought to herself . . . weird indeed! What a bizarre nightmare she was having.

Chapter 10

Ganga took Radhika to a small room in one wing of the palace. It was one of about a dozen rooms in which most of the girls slept in pairs or three to a room. They slept on straw-stuffed pallets upon the ground, and the only furniture in each room was a small table with a mirror upon it. Each girl had a trunk, in which she kept her clothes and personal items.

Ganga fetched a pallet for Radhika to sleep on, along with a pillow and two sheets, one to be spread below and one to cover herself with.

'Tomorrow, we'll get the rest of your luggage from wherever you were staying,' she said, indicating that Radhika make herself at home. She didn't know what made her lie to Ganga, but Radhika found herself telling Ganga that she had been robbed of all her luggage and had none. Ganga looked sympathetically at her.

'What about the person you had come to see?' she asked.

'They were not there. I am totally alone and lost,' said Radhika.

'Oh, you poor thing!' exclaimed Ganga and hugged her. 'Never mind. I'll lend you some of my clothes and ask the Rani Sahiba to give you some advance from your stipend to buy new clothes tomorrow. You cannot possibly remain in these clothes that you're wearing. Now go to sleep.'

Radhika removed her sneakers and lay down upon the pallet, thinking she would never sleep after all the bizarre happenings. But she must have slept off immediately, because the next thing she knew, Ganga was shaking her awake.

'What time is it?' mumbled Radhika, without opening her eyes, as she stretched out a hand for the alarm clock that she kept on a small table beside her bed. As her hand met nothing but air, she suddenly remembered where she was. Her eyes shot open and she found Ganga shaking her. She held a lamp in her hand as it was still pitch dark. Radhika looked around and felt sick to find herself still where she had dropped off to sleep and not in her bed at Noida.

'It is the first *pahar*, sister. You must finish with your daily ablutions, and then we have to report in the courtyard for our daily yoga session,' Ganga explained.

Radhika scrambled up, wondering if for answering the call of nature, they would be going into the fields, which was true even today in some parts of rural India despite the massive efforts of the government to address this issue.

Radhika found herself walking through the palace towards one end where the toilets were located. The night before, she had been in too much of a shock to observe anything, but now she noticed that they passed through well-maintained passages from which various chambers opened out. She managed to peep into some but could not make out much as the only light was provided by the lantern held by Ganga. They crossed two courtyards and came to another, around which there were many small chambers. There was a well in the centre of the courtyard, with two women on duty to pull up water.

To her surprise, she found that the toilet arrangements were quite modern, considering the time was supposed to be the middle of the eighteenth century. Half the tiny rooms had a raised platform inside with a hole in it that obviously led down into a deep pit. You had to squat over it, very much like you did on the Indian toilet still in use in India. The only thing was that there was no white porcelain used here. But the toilets were clean and not smelly. Each room had a bucket of water kept along with a *lota*. Outside the rooms sat a maid with another bucket of water and a *lota* and with some fresh *mitti*, or earth, and helped you wash your hands.

For brushing, neem twigs were provided along with more water and with another maid to help. The water was continuously replenished by the maids from a well.

The other small rooms were provided with buckets of water and *lotas* for everyone to take a bath.

Radhika was impressed.

After having finished with their ablutions, Ganga and she, along with quite a few other young maidens, went along to another, bigger courtyard. Here, the rani presided over their yoga class.

After forty-five minutes of yoga, they all had to go along to another courtyard, which had been covered from the side. Here, there was an *akhara*. To Radhika's surprise, the rani herself, dressed in the Maharashtrian type of *dhoti saari*, picked one of her ladies in waiting who was similarly dressed and the two of them started wrestling. After five minutes, she asked everyone to choose a partner and follow her. Very soon, there were at least ten pairs of ladies wrestling on the dirt floor of the courtyard. The rani would demonstrate a hold and the other ladies would follow her. Radhika was amazed at the expertise demonstrated by some of them.

Radhika asked Ganga who had trained the rani. Ganga said that the *guru ji* from Bithoor had come and demonstrated all the holds to the rani, who now taught them to her entourage.

It being Radhika's first day, she had been spared and stood on one side, watching with an open mouth. To imagine women wrestling in those days! Once they had finished, the rani came up to her and asked her how she had liked the demonstration.

'I liked it a lot and am very surprised, Rani Sahiba,' said Radhika.

'Would you like to learn?' asked the rani.

'I already know self-defence and some karate,' said Radhika.

'And what is that?' asked the rani, looking interested.

Radhika explained. The rani asked her to demonstrate it. Radhika got down into the *akhara*. She picked two of the heftiest-looking wrestlers, Sona and Meera, and asked them to rush her from both sides. When the two women rushed her simultaneously, she tackled Sona by simply bending down, shoving her left shoulder into Sona's solar plexus, dropping her head and hands to hold Sona behind the knees, and throwing her over her left shoulder, mostly using Sona's momentum to her own advantage. Then, whirling around, she put her right foot behind Meera, punched through the gap between Meera's right shoulder and ear and shoved her backward, toppling Meera over her right foot. Then, as the two women lay winded, she walked away, smiling. There was thunderous applause. The rani looked impressed. She came and clapped Radhika on her back and asked her how she would like to train her women in this new kind of art of fighting. Radhika agreed delightedly.

After wrestling, it was the time for another martial art of India, *malkhamb*. In this, the women climbed up a greased pole with just their bare hands and feet.

There was a greased wooden pillar at one end of the courtyard. They all had a try at it, so what if many fell down badly. They just dusted themselves and tried again. Many ended up with bruises.

After all this exercise, the women were sweaty and tired. The rani sent them back for another bath. Then she held prayers with them for fifteen minutes and sent them for breakfast while she continued her own prayers for another half an hour or so.

Breakfast was a hearty meal of *poori* and vegetables and cool *lassi*. It was only after this that the ladies went about the rest of their daily chores.

Radhika was at a loss after breakfast and wondering what she was supposed to do. She had also begun to wonder which year it was. There did not seem to be any calendars around. She had by now realised that going by the apparent age of the child she had seen the night before, she had landed up somewhere in 1856 or 57, just before the rebellion had taken place. Just then, one of the girls came to call her. The rani had partaken of her spartan breakfast, consisting of some milk and fruit, and was asking for her. Her heart almost skipped a beat. Then she hurried after the girl who had come to call her.

Chapter 11

Radhika and her escort left the palace and went outside. After crossing a huge courtyard, they came to another, smaller building. This was the library-cum-study. Here, there were a few tables with chairs scattered around. The walls of the room were lined with shelves full of books and rolled up manuscripts and journals. A few scholars sat around, copying from manuscripts by hand. She was shown into a smaller, separate room, where the rani waited for her.

To her surprise, she found that the rani knew the rudiments of English quite well. In fact, she was well past the primary level and now could formulate full sentences. She was now rather keen to learn how to write a letter, how to address the dignitaries of the East India Company, and how to write to the Queen of England, whom she was most keen to communicate with. She also wanted to practice how to speak proper English. She had set aside an hour every day for this task with Radhika. In a way, Radhika was happy but also not very sure where all this was leading to. She was also beginning to wonder how long she would have to stay in this time warp. This nightmare of hers seemed to just go on, with no end in view. Would she be stuck here forever? The very thought scared her.

The rani was an intelligent and hard-working pupil. She picked up things very fast. Radhika was surprised at her knowledge of what was going on in the world at that time. Especially with no radios, TV, or Internet. The rani was especially interested in the latest scientific discoveries. Radhika realised that many of the things that she had taken for granted in her life had yet to be discovered. One of those was the ballpoint pen. The rani used quills made out of bird feathers, dipping a sharpened end in a pot of ink and writing. Radhika had heard that her great-grandmother used to use a quill to write with. She had seen some quills in museums but had never imagined that she would actually see someone using one to write with. She found it fascinating.

After the class was over, the rani went back to her chambers to take a look at her son, while Radhika was led back to where the other girls were using their free time to do whatever they pleased. Some were repairing their clothes, others were writing home, and yet others were reading or just sitting around talking. Ganga immediately took her along to another room in the palace, where there were about a dozen seamstresses busy stitching clothes for all the royal maids. Here, Ganga caught hold of the head seamstress.

'Amma, do you have any clothes ready? My friend Radhika here needs some immediately.'

The old woman frowned at Ganga. 'You are forever in a hurry, Ganga Bai. All I hear is immediately, immediately, and more immediately from you. I only have two hands and two eyes and only a limited number of girls working for me,' she grumbled.

'Come on, Amma,' said Ganga. 'Radhika's entire luggage was stolen, and she is the latest addition to the Maharani Sahiba's entourage. So, the clothes better be ready immediately.'

At the mention of the rani, the old woman raised an eyebrow. Then, she pursed her lips. She gave Radhika a once-over, muttering under her breath about strange people and stranger clothes. Turning around, she opened a large wooden box placed behind her. She rummaged through it and produced a pair of red and green *lehengas* with matching *cholies*.

'She cannot ride or do exercise in those, Amma!' protested Ganga.

The old woman looked mutinous. Then, she finally produced two *nauvaris*, along with their *cholies*.

'But how will I tie them?' asked Radhika in dismay. She could hardly tie a normal *saree*, leave alone a traditional nine-yard-long Maharashtrian version.

Ganga smiled at her. 'Don't worry. I'll teach you.'

So, they left the sewing room with the two *sarees* and their accompanying *cholies*.

The next hour was spent in Ganga teaching Radhika how to tie a nine-yard version of what she called a *dhoti saree*. Some of the other girls also joined in, and Radhika had a sneaky feeling that they all were enjoying her discomfiture. They all were curious about Radhika: where was she from and how she had come to be recruited to be one of them. They had, of course, heard the story of how she had tackled the would-be assassin and were quite impressed by it. They also wondered why she had on such odd clothes and were especially curious about her undergarments, the likes of which they had never seen. They examined each one as it was revealed and could not understand what some of them were for, especially the unmentionable for the upper portion of the body. They examined her jeans also as they had not seen that kind of cloth.

For their riding class, they all insisted that Radhika wear one of her new dresses. Radhika felt rather shy as she walked with them to the huge garden just below the library, where the rani taught them not only riding but also how to handle a sword while riding, how to stand up in the saddle and shoot arrows, etc. It was an experience for her. The rani herself would sometimes hold the rein in her teeth and plying a sword in each hand, take on more than one of her friends at the same time. The ladies also had jousting practice. Here, they were joined by some more women from the town.

Radhika had to confess that she had done some riding but it was the bare minimum. The rani assigned a soft, rather tame, horse named Surajmukhi to her. She was really a sweety pie and very soon, Radhika was also cantering round the courtyard with the others confidently enough. Of course, although Radhika was longing to try her hand at sword fighting, she needed both her hands to manage the mare as she was still too new.

After riding, the rani went in for some rest while all her ladies had some free time to do what they liked. Ganga introduced Radhika around to more of the girls. Lunch was simple, consisting of rice, *daal*, and two vegetables, and after that, it was siesta time till evening, when there was another bout of exercising. Really, the rani did believe in keeping not only herself but also all her companions fit. This was followed by a reading from one of the sacred scriptures for one hour and then a simple dinner of a curry with *chapattis*. After this, the rani went to personally supervise putting her son Damodar Rao, whom she had adopted after the death of her real son, to bed and then she retired for the night, as did all her lady companions.

As Radhika lay on her pallet that night, she was surprised that a whole day had gone by. She wondered what her family in Noida would be doing and what they would be thinking about her sudden disappearance. Would they have informed the police? This was a bizarre adventure she was having, and if she ever went back, she was sure no one would believe her. Just the thought that she might never go back suddenly made her feel very lonely. She could feel her eyes brimming over, and then silent tears were coursing down her cheeks and wetting her straw pillow.

Suddenly, she felt someone's arm going around her. It was Ganga, who cuddled her and patting her back, murmured consolingly, 'There, there, my dear. Missing your family? We all do in the beginning. But then, you learn to enjoy here.'

Radhika sobbed for a long time in the comforting arms of Ganga and never realised when she finally fell asleep still cuddled up in them.

Chapter 12

Next day, the rani brought her son with her for her English class.

'I want you to teach him English also. He must know it so that he can communicate with the *firangis* himself and not be dependent on anyone,' she told her.

Radhika was surprised. She had never read anywhere that Damodar Rao had been taught English, but apparently, he had been.

The day was like any other. After breakfast, the rani dressed herself in pyjamas and a *kurta* and tied a sword on either side. She even took two pistols and carried a shield upon her back. She wore an iron helmet covered with a golden scarf and went out riding. She asked her three favourite friends, along with Ganga and Radhika, to accompany her. Radhika thought she wanted to show her the terrain around Jhansi.

It was while they were riding outside the town when they heard the sound of firing. They all halted and looked at each other. Then, the rani turned her horse in the direction of the sound and they raced towards it. They rounded a huge *tekri* and came across a strange sight. Some women out cutting grass had put down their bundles upon the ground and were now lying on the ground and using rifles to shoot at a boulder painted red. One woman was directing them. She was obviously their instructor. On spotting the rani, they respectfully stopped the firing and got up. The rani halted and addressed all of them in a familiar way. It turned out that they all belonged to her *nari sena*, Durga Dal. Their leader seemed someone whom the rani addressed as Jhalkari. Radhika got a shock when Jhalkari turned and joined her hands in front of the rani. The woman was especially very well dressed and wearing a lot of jewellery, all made out of silver. The surprising thing was that the woman bore an uncanny resemblance to the rani. Of a similar build, she had a regal look about her. Only she was darker in colour. But immediately she opened her mouth, her uncouth language gave her away.

The rani asked her how their shooting practice was going on. It turned out that Jhalkari was one of the leaders of the *nari sena* of the rani and was trying to train other women from the town in shooting as the rani had wanted her to do this. The rani was very pleased with her. She praised all of them, and soon, once again, they all were cantering out in the wilderness. As they rode away, Radhika asked Ganga who Jhalkari was.

'She is one of the best shots we have in the *nari army*,' said Ganga.

'Did you see how much she looked like the Rani Sahiba?' commented Radhika.

'Yes. She is nearly as brave. She belongs to the Kori caste. They are untouchables, but she is an only child and lost her mother when she was very young. She is not educated in the real sense but is well versed in the use of arms. You know, once she killed a leopard with just a stick when it attacked her. And once, when dacoits attacked her village, she fought them bravely and ran them off. Then she got married to Puran Singh, a soldier in the rani's army. Rani

Sahiba has made her in charge of teaching the other women of the lower castes how to use all sorts of weapons,' said Ganga to the surprised Radhika.

They all rode around for more than an hour and then returned. The rani immediately retired to the library, where she had pulled out some paper maps from some shelves at the back. She pored over these and added a mark or two on them. Radhika peeped over her shoulders and realised that the map she was poring over was a map of Jhansi and the area around it. It had been no ordinary ride the rani had gone on. In the garb of taking exercise, she had been noting down every big rock, *tekri*, and anything else that could give help to any force trying to approach Jhansi stealthily. She had been making herself familiar with every inch of land in and around Jhansi. Seeing Radhika looking, the rani smiled at her and explained that this would come in handy in defending Jhansi later on, when fighting broke out.

Besides riding out often, the rani had intensified the training of her ladies' army. She insisted that each and every one not only kept herself fit by exercise and yoga but also practiced riding, self-defence, fighting with a sword, and firing a gun. Some of them wanted to learn how to fire the bigger artillery guns. The rani promised to give them training for that also.

The rani was very particular about her lessons in English. She seldom missed a day. Now, she had taken to bringing her son along to every lesson in English. Damodar was a friendly boy, and when the rani realised that he liked Radhika, she told Radhika to take him under her wing and talk to him in English always so that he learnt it fast.

Radhika was happy to oblige her. She loved looking after the little boy, who was rather well behaved for a child his age. With no recourse to too many English books, she took to drawing in the mud to explain things to him. Generally, after the English lesson with his mother and Radhika, he would drag Radhika to the garden below the library and wanted her to play with him there. At night, he insisted on hearing a story or two from her. Radhika supposed the rani would have liked her to tell him religious or mythological stories but unfortunately, she knew very few of them. She and her brother had been fans of comics.

By now, Radhika was sure that she had landed up in the time when the rebellion was being planned. There had been a lot of clandestine activity going on. Many mysterious people came to visit the rani late at night so that they could meet her and go away undetected. These men came with their faces covered and were immediately granted an audience with the rani, whatever the time of the night or day it was. Generally, these meetings were very hush hush and the rani was only attended by three or four of her immediate best ladies: Sunder, Munder, Ganga and Kashi Bai. But for some meetings, even Radhika was allowed to attend. In fact, she had been there hardly a week when the evening meal was interrupted by the female guards on duty outside. Generally, the rani took this meal with all of her ladies. The female sentry gave a discreet cough at the door. When the rani told her to enter, the sentry informed her that there were some men who had come and wanted an urgent audience with her. The rani immediately left her food and after washing her hands went out. Sunder, Munder, Kashi Bai , Ganga, and Radhika followed her. They found two men with faces covered waiting in a room. In the beginning, they looked questioningly at the girls but the rani sat down upon a chair and told them, 'You can talk in front of these girls. They are all loyal to me personally. And outside, there is a strict guard of females. No one will disturb us.'

Then only did the men take off their masks. They turned out to be Tatya Tope and a man named Bhaktiar.

'Tatya Guru, please give me all the report about where all you have been and how ready the general public is to start the rebellion,' said the Rani quietly.

'Bai Saheb, I visited the Punjab, but there is little hope from there. The maharaja is young and his mother rules instead. The public also seems to be indifferent. The same goes for Rajasthan. But the scene in Uttar Pradesh and Madhya Pradesh is very different. At Delhi, not only have the British stopped all that was offered as *nazarana* to the *badshah* for the past ten or twelve years but now want the Mughal emperor to vacate Red Fort and move to Munger so that the British can rule from Delhi. The Muslims are very, very angry at this.'

'The *firangis* came as supplicants and now have made themselves masters,' said the second man in disgust.

'And the controversy about the contaminated cartridges for the rifles is getting stronger by the day. People in Calcutta asked some people who worked in the factories where the cartridges were made and they confirmed that huge tenders had been given to people to supply animal grease from cows and pigs for the manufacture of these cartridges. And it is rumoured that before the cartridges can be used, the sepoys will have to bite off the papers on these with their teeth,' added Tatya in anger.

'But we all are not yet ready for the start of the rebellion,' said the rani. 'I have found people who can manufacture artillery guns that do not ricochet too much and men who can make almost smokeless gunpowder. But we need time to set up things in place and prepare the people for the rebellion. We want the rebellion to start at the same time all over Bharat '

'I agree with you, Bai Saheb. But the people are restless and chomping at the bit. How long they will be able to hold on to their patience is questionable. Every day, the British insult them in some way or the other. They have taken over all the lucrative jobs and given them only the most menial and underpaid ones. They treat the Indians like slaves and expect them to be thankful for it to boot,' said Tatya bitterly.

'But we have to hold on. An early, unprepared rising would be fatal. Our soldiers would die needlessly, and the rebellion would fail,' said the rani desperately.

The two men nodded. They discussed other things now. The 31st of May was chosen as the big date. 'That is the season for the lotus flower to blossom in profusion in our local ponds. One lotus flower, along with one fresh *roti*, will be circulated from village to village as the signal for the rebellion to begin,' said the rani. 'Religious figures, like *sadhus*, will be the carriers. Only then will the rebellion start all over Bharat on the same day and at the same time,' ended the rani. The two men nodded, then took their leave to spread this message, and vanished into the night.

The girls all went back to their interrupted dinner, but the rani only drank a glass of warm milk and then retired for the night.

Chapter 13

But things were not to run smoothly. Before long, there was an incident at Barrackpore, near Calcutta. A sweeper asked a Brahmin sepoy to give him water to drink from his *lota*. The sepoy refused. The sweeper taunted him saying that the very *dharam* the sepoy was trying to preserve by refusing him, the sweeper, water would not last very long when the new cartridges greased with the tallow from cows and pigs came into use and sepoys would have to use their teeth to open them. This incident started a riot, and the British court-martialled the Brahmin sepoy and hanged him. To further rub salt into the wounds, they forced all the Hindu sepoys to witness this and made them lay down their arms.

Soon after this, once the lotuses had bloomed, holy men started circulating from village to village taking the flower and a fresh *roti* and informing the people that the 31st of May was the date fixed for the rebellion to begin. Every day, the rani was getting news about where all the signal had been forwarded. But before this transfer of message had completed its full circuit, on the 6th of May, another incident rocked Meerut. The rani got the news that out of ninety sepoys who had been issued the new cartridges supposed to be greased with the tallow from cows and pigs, eighty-five had refused to use them. They were immediately court-martialled, stripped off their uniforms and arms, and put in irons. Other Indian sepoys were made to witness this. This took place in the morning. In the evening, some of the sepoys went into the local bazaar and were heckled by some prostitutes and then by some families. This was intolerable to them. They returned and held a conference that night, deciding that they would not wait till the 31st to start the rebellion. They would kill their British officers and march to Delhi. They sent a message to Delhi. Next morning, while the British were at church, the sepoys murdered their officers and their families and started for Delhi, where they joined with the troops there. They acknowledged Bahadur Shah as the emperor of India and gave him a twenty-one-gun salute.

Messages regarding this break out reached Jhansi. Radhika could see that the rani was very upset about it. 'It is premature. We are not ready for it yet. It will cost us dear!' she exclaimed in distress. 'Don't allow anyone to come to see me,' she ordered.

Obviously, the news reached the British in Jhansi also. Gordon, who was the deputy commissioner, immediately withdrew with the families into the fort for safety. Unfortunately, the fort, which was a little outside Jhansi, was not too well stocked.

∧∧∧∧∧∧∧∧∧∧∧

A few days later, late at night, Gordon suddenly demanded an audience with the rani. The rani, who had been about to sit down to her dinner, got up immediately and went out. Sunder, Munder, Ganga and Radhika followed her. The deputy commissioner was very agitated. Apparently, mutiny had broken out in Cawnpore also and some soldiers were marching towards Jhansi.

'I don't fear for us, Rani Sahiba. We will supress it. But I fear for the families who are in town. I request you to give them shelter in your palace.'

Immediately they heard this, Munder placed a hand upon the shoulder of the rani. She whispered into her ears that it would be best to avoid such a commitment. It could lead to a lot of trouble. The rani looked at her and replied softly.

'Munder, we are fighting the British soldiers. Our fight is not with their women and children. Tell him he can bring the families for shelter here.'

Munder frowned and would have argued, but the rani gave her a quelling look and she subsided. The rani turned to Radhika and told her to tell Gordon what she had said. Although Radhika did not agree with the rani, she told Mr. Gordon what the rani had said. Mr. Gordon smiled gratefully and turning raced out.

Within an hour, all the British families had arrived. Radhika and Munder were put in charge of looking after them as they both knew English and could communicate with them.

But things had not finished yet. The families were fed and sleeping arrangements were being made for them when another message came. The commissioner, Mr. Skeen, had decided against leaving the families under the protection of the rani and wanted her to send them to Star Fort, where the British army had shifted. It was obvious he did not trust the rani.

Without any protest, the rani sent all the families under escort to Star Fort, where the British had retreated, and they closed the gates. The families had left in haste, leaving behind quite a lot of their personal baggage. Radhika and Ganga cleared up behind them. It was while they were clearing up that Radhika came across a small loose-leaf journal in which obviously some lady had been writing. To her surprise, it turned out not to be a diary but a bunch of short stories. As she went through it that night, she found it to be a real bonanza, a treasure trove of short stories. She realised that now she would be able to tell the young yuvraj many more stories and not limit herself to those of Indian mythology only. That journal contained stories about pirates, sailors, robbers like Robin Hood, who robbed the rich and gave to the poor, buried treasure, etc. Now she started telling the little boy these stories. Damodar was fascinated with the idea of finding buried treasure belonging to some long-dead sailor. It had taken Radhika some time to explain to him what exactly a pirate was as he had no idea what a sea or an ocean was. Radhika had discovered some good maps of the world in the library and used these to explain things to the enchanted, round-eyed child, who immediately decided that when he grew up, he would not become the Maharaja of Jhansi but a pirate upon the high sea and rob people.

'Then, I will bury all the treasure I gather,' he stated firmly, making Radhika smile.

Unfortunately, inside Star Fort, as it was called because of its formation, there was little food or ammunition. Two days later, the rani got the news that all the food in the fort had finished and the families were starving. To Radhika's utter surprise, the rani ordered two mounds of *rotis* made and then told Sunder, Munder, Kashi, and

Radhika to go by a secret tunnel that went from outside Star Fort to inside it and deliver the food to the families there.

'But why are you doing this, ma'am?' Radhika asked the rani. 'They are the enemy. You should let them starve.'

The rani smiled at her. 'What a hot head you are, Radhika. No. I will win over them in a fair fight. I refuse to fight a starving enemy. And, I do not fight women and children. It is unethical and my *dharam* does not allow me to do so.'

Munder, who was standing there, muttered under her breath, 'If it was the other way around, I am sure the British would have no compunction in killing our women and children.'

'You said something?' the rani asked Munder in a cold voice.

'No, Rani Sahiba,' muttered Munder and looked a little ashamed.

Radhika too felt the rebuke but all she could do was nod silently. The rani really was a noble soul.

Chapter 14

Sunder, Munder, Kashi Bai, and Radhika left in the dead of night. They left Jhansi by a secret tunnel that ran from near one of the gates to the outside. All of them carried the *rotis* tied in cloth upon their backs. Star Fort was about a mile or two outside Jhansi. Munder knew the way, and as there was a half-moon, it was not very difficult finding their way there. They stopped just short of the fort, where there was a dry riverbed. Here, Munder pushed aside a bush and revealed a small wooden door in the side of the hill. This door was not latched, and she pulled it open. They found themselves in a rocky tunnel that seemed to be going uphill. Sunder produced a small lamp, and Radhika had carried her torch. The other girls, when they had first seen it, had been very curious and fascinated with it as they had never seen one. They were fascinated by how with just the push of a switch, it lit up or went off. They all had wanted to play with it. Fortunately, it was one of those that could be hand cranked and had a mini generator that could charge it, and its battery could be recharged without being replaced. Many of the girls had spent hours cranking the generator and seeing the bulb light up, and they all had been like children with a fascinating new toy. But they had gotten used to it very fast.

It was obvious that the tunnel was a secret entrance into Star Fort. The passage had been hewn from the hillside itself and then shored up with rocks. At places, it was narrow and musty but they managed to continue. After half an hour, they came to another door and on opening it, found themselves in a deserted courtyard in the old part of Star Fort.

Radhika could see sentries walking up and down on duty on the ramparts of the fort. 'Let us ask for Mr. Gordon, the deputy commissioner,' she suggested.

'Yes,' agreed Munder. 'Others might not know us and be suspicious of us.'

Suddenly, one of the sentries spotted them and called out, 'Who goes there? Password please!'

'We have come from the palace of Rani Laxmi Bai,' called out Radhika. 'She has sent us. We would like to see Deputy Commissioner Gordon.'

There was an exclamation of surprise, and then two sentries came charging down a staircase from the rampart. They carried guns on the ready. They waved the guns at the girls dangerously, and it took some convincing on the girls' part to make them believe that they had really come from the palace. The sentries made them take off the bags upon their backs and checked them and were surprised to find them full of food only. Then only did they take them to see Mr. Gordon, who had been woken up by now. He was equally surprised to see the girls. At first, he also looked puzzled, but then he looked grateful and told them to thank the rani for her generosity. After this, the four of them went back the same way they had come.

The next night, they did the same thing. But this time, the British were ready for them. They eagerly grabbed the food and thanked them. When they were returning,

Radhika didn't know why she felt a little uneasy. She felt as if someone was following them. She kept turning back to look, but there was no one. What she didn't know was that one of the British soldiers had actually followed the girls and on discovering the secret passage, he had got out of the fort that night and gone off for help to Agra.

In Jhansi, the rani heard reports that the situation in the fort was deteriorating. It was not the lack of food only. There were no medicines. Even water was in short supply. The British were dying like flies.

It was the 8th of July. A lot of disturbance was heard in Jhansi town. As the sound grew, the sentries shut the gates of the palace. A big contingent of rebel sepoys had entered the town and, standing in front of the palace, were demanding an audience with the rani. The rani came out on her balcony and stood with folded hands. All her ladies stood behind her, fully armed and at the ready. Radhika, who was standing with them, could feel the nervousness in everyone. The soldiers looked belligerent and aggressive. They looked more like raiders than any disciplined soldiers. The rani addressed them in a strong voice, 'Who are you all, and why are you attacking Jhansi? Who is your leader?'

'I am,' said a fierce looking man, stepping forward. 'I am risaldar Kale Khan. We are coming from Star Fort and planning to go to Delhi to join the *fauj* there.'

'Why are your swords stained with blood? What has happened to the British families who were in the Fort?' asked the rani.

'Today, they surrendered to us. They wanted to come here for shelter under you. On the way here, we took them to Jokhan Bagh and killed them all,' said Kale Khan.

The rani looked horrified. 'By whose orders did you kill them?' she demanded sharply.

'By no one's order. They deserved to die,' said Kale Khan.

'You know what you have done is a very cowardly act! Killing unarmed families. Is this what soldiering has taught you all?' demanded the rani angrily.

Some of the men looked ashamed of themselves, but others looked defiant. They started whispering amongst themselves.

Anger suffused the rani's face. 'Have you no shame of any sort? Where has all the discipline taught to you gone? Have you forgotten all your honour?'

There was a murmur amongst the gathered rebels.

At last, Kale Khan looked up at her. 'I am sorry for what happened today morning, Rani Sahiba, but now nothing can be done about it. From now on, nothing will be done unless you order it. We will obey your orders and do whatever you say.'

'Then go back to your barracks. The time has not yet come for the rebellion to start,' said the rani.

Immediately, there was a hullabaloo amongst the standing rebels. Some of them started saying, 'If we go back, we'll all be killed. She seems to have no sympathy for us or our cause. Let us get some money from her and go to Delhi. If she does not give us money, let us loot the city of Jhansi.'

Kale Khan at last looked up at the rani. 'The sepoys want to go to Delhi, Rani Sahiba. But we need money. If you cannot give us the money, we will have to raise it from the town.' The rani looked disgusted. She realised that the soldiers were fast running out of patience. If she did not do something soon, they would loot her beloved Jhansi. She took off the diamond necklace she wore around her neck and threw it to Kale khan.

'Sell this and raise the money you need. It should be enough. Now go peacefully like disciplined soldiers and not riff-raff.'

The soldiers raised slogans in praise of the rani and then turned and marched out under Kale Khan. The rani turned and, returning to her room, collapsed in her chair. It had been a close call, but she had managed to save her beloved Jhansi from being looted and put to torch. Everyone was still stunned about what had taken place at Jokhan Bagh.

'Why are soldiers so cruel?' asked Ganga in anguish.

'They killed Gordon sahib and all the *firangis*. Horrible!' ejaculated Kashi Bai.

'I can't believe they killed all the women and children also!' exclaimed Radhika angrily.

'Rani Sahiba is furious,' said Munder.

'Yes. It is totally against her principals,' said Sunder.

'There are devils in every army,' observed Ganga, looking disgusted.

'I don't mind killing in a fair fight, but to kill in cold blood . . .' Munder looked upset. She was not the only one. All of them were upset. The thought of the young children whom they had seen just a few days before and fed and sheltered and now who had been killed most brutally when they were least expecting it made them all feel sick.

Chapter 15

The rani called an immediate meeting of all the leaders of the communities in the town. As usual, Radhika also stood along with the other girls behind the rani. The rani sat behind a thin curtain. Very soon, a heated discussion was going on. Leaders from various communities of the business class, like the *telis* and the *banias*, were vociferous. The rani asked if she should inform the British residents at Cawnpore about the rebellion of the sepoys and say that there was no rebellion in Jhansi and that she was in control there. There was an immediate protest from all the leaders of the various communities. They were of the opinion that the British had got their just deserts and had been removed at last. Why should they be told that their rule was still on? The people wanted their own beloved rani to rule.

'Why should we invite the devils back now that they have been thrown out at last,' protested one leader.

'We have just managed to throw off their yolk. It would be madness to invite them back to come and sit upon our heads once again,' said another.

'But we are not ready for the rebellion,' said the rani.

'Yes. It would be better to pretend that Rani Sahiba is still holding and ruling Jhansi in the name of the British *sarkar*, just in case things fail,' agreed her father, Moropant.

'In this way, we can go on preparing for the rebellion and when the rebellion finally breaks out, if it succeeds, Rani Sahiba gets her beloved Jhansi back and even if it fails, she still remains in charge of it,' said another senior leader.

After a lot of argument, very reluctantly, the city leaders agreed for the rani to send a message to the British residents at Cawnpore with the news of the massacre at Jokhan Bagh. After the city leaders had left, the rani held a private meeting with her top *sardars*. The wordings of the letter to be sent to the residents at Cawnpore were decided upon. After the *sardars* had left, the rani sat down with Radhika and drafted a letter informing the residents at Cawnpore about the massacre at Jokhan Bagh. Then she wrote that it was done without her knowledge and that she had barely managed to save Jhansi from being torched and looted as there were not enough soldiers in her army for its defence. Now, the rebels had left for Delhi and she was holding Jhansi and ruling it in the name of the British. She also requested permission to recruit more soldiers in her army to be able to defend Jhansi from further attacks of this sort.

The people were not happy with the fact that they had been told to be patient. To them, it seemed that this was a golden opportunity that the rani was not utilising.

∧∧∧∧∧∧∧∧∧∧∧

It was a few days later. The monsoon broke. Incessant rain started falling. All the rivers around Jhansi became raging torrents. The girls were all having their dinner when news came that a famous dacoit by the name of Sagar Singh, who had been the terror of Baruasagar, was holed up in his *haveli* in his village. Sagar Singh had been indulging in a lot of looting and dacoity and was wanted by the British. He had been captured once and had got away from their jail and now generally hid in deep forests. The rani sent for Khuda Baksh to apprehend him and bring him in dead or alive. Khuda Baksh, at one time, had been a favourite of Gangadhar Rao's, but because of taking interest in the raja's favourite dancer, he had been banished from Jhansi and all his land confiscated. Once Gangadhar Rao passed away, the rani allowed him to return and helped him regain his lands. He was always grateful to her for that.

'Will you be able to do it?' she questioned Khuda Baksh anxiously when he arrived.

'Definitely,' said Khuda Baksh emphatically.

'If you need more men, take them. Look for the dacoit at his *addas*. The villagers are on his side and usually help him,' said the Rani.

'I don't think I'll require more men. If required, I'll let your majesty know,' replied Khuda Baksh.

∧∧∧∧∧∧∧∧∧∧∧

A few days later, they got the news that Khuda Baksh had surrounded the house of the dacoit where he had been residing in the village but the man had got away and in the fight that had ensued, Gul Mohammad had been badly injured.

The rani called all the girls and informed them about this. At that time, Moti Bai, the courtesan, was with her, rendering some *bhajans*. On hearing that Gul Mohammad was injured, she paled visibly. The rani looked at her and patted her hand reassuringly. Then, turning to the other girls, she asked, 'How many of you are willing to ride out with me right now? It is raining heavily.'

They all looked at her questioningly.

She smiled at them. 'I plan to take a hand in apprehending this dacoit myself. I was thinking of taking some of you and going after the man myself.'

All of the girls were keen to go along. The rani decided to leave Kashi Bai behind to look after administrative matters while she took most of the others and some male soldiers along with her. Moti Bai also insisted on accompanying her. They all knew that Moti Bai, although a courtesan, was in love with Gul Mohammad and nothing on earth would have kept her from his side when he was injured.

It was an experience for Radhika to be racing on a horse through pouring rain, which nearly blinded her, and being completely dependent on her horse and its instincts to keep her safe. They all came to the river Betawa. To their dismay, they found it in spate. It was no longer a shallow river but a raging torrent. The boat men found it impossible to launch any boats to cross it. The rani looked at her troops. She then told them that they would have to cross the river on foot. She ordered them to hold their guns and packs of gunpowder over their heads while doing so to avoid damaging them. Then, she plunged into the raging torrent and struck out for the other shore, leading her horse behind her by his reins. Seeing her, all the others followed suit. The shock of the force of the water swept most of them off their feet and they had to swim for their lives. At one point, Radhika nearly gave up. All her strength seemed to have drained from her body. But the next moment, someone was holding on to her and dragging her behind them. That person dragged her the last twenty yards or so and as they crawled out onto the other side, Radhika realised it was the rani herself who had dragged her out.

They all lay there on the other side with their equally exhausted horses for quite some time. Fortunately, the sky had cleared and in the ensuing sunshine, their clothes dried out fast. To their delight, their gunpowder and guns were still dry. After some time, they made their way to the village where the battle between Gul Mohammad and Sagar Singh had taken place. They found Gul Mohammad lying badly injured in the house that had been occupied by Sagar Singh. The rani left Moti Bai to look after him and after a hasty meal, they all moved towards the jungle where an informer had told them Sagar Singh was hiding.

They reached the hillock upon which he had camped and realised that they would have to attack in the open with no cover. It would be suicidal as the dacoits would immediately spot them. The rani distributed her men and women into four groups, and they all approached the hillock simultaneously. There was no way Sagar Singh could escape now, although the fight would be fierce. Radhika and Munder were with the rani along with two male soldiers. They were halfway up the hillock when they heard a rustling sound. Suddenly, a rider broke cover and raced down straight towards their group. He was better dressed than the average dacoit and even wore some jewellery. The rani decided that the man met the description given to her of Sagar Singh. She made a signal by hand to her group and turning her horse gave chase. Radhika realised that if they had been making a feature film, she would have probably been shown shouting out an order to chase the man but in reality, when you are riding hard on the ground, the sound from the flying feet of your steed drowns out any sound and makes it impossible for anyone to be heard. So, hand signals have to be used. This was a new lesson for her.

They all immediately turned their horses and gave chase. The rani and Munder were far ahead of all of the others. Radhika saw that as they started rapidly catching up with the rider, he burst through the cordon. As they came abreast, the rani nodded to Munder, who nodded back, having understood immediately what was wanted. Both women galloped alongside the galloping dacoit. They stretched out one arm each, and the next moment they had plucked off the dacoit from his racing horse, which raced off without his rider, while the two women held the man in an iron grip. The two slowed down and jumped off their horses, pushing the struggling man, who had not been armed, to the ground.

The others all reached them, and the four male soldiers with them quickly jumped down and tied up the man, who by now they were sure was Sagar Singh. The rani got the bugler to blow his bugle so that all the other parties could return. The other dacoits got away.

They took Sagar Singh back to the village, where he was brought in front of the rani next morning.

'Are you Sagar Singh?' asked the Rani.

'Kunwar Sagar Singh,' replied the dacoit arrogantly.

'You call yourself Kunwar and seem to come from landed gentry. Why have you taken to looting and pillaging?' asked the Rani.

'*Sarkar*, our family has always taken part in wars. We have fought in the army of the Maharaja of Orchha. We fought alongside Maharaj Chhatrasal. But when the British came, we were amongst those who refused to serve under them. When they started harassing us, we also retaliated and became rebels. I can swear on my own behalf and that of my associates that we never looted or troubled women, children, or the poor.'

'These days, the people you are harassing are all my subjects, not of the British. The punishment for dacoity is death. Get ready for it. Neither will any of your associates escape. I am going to raze all your dwellings to the ground.'

The man looked at the rani arrogantly and then threw back his head and said, 'There is only one request, *sarkar*.'

'Speak,' said the rani.

'Put me to death by either a bullet or a sword. If you hang me, it will be an insult to my lineage and dacoity will only increase.'

The rani looked thoughtful and asked, 'And if I leave you, what will you do?'

Sagar Singh looked taken aback. 'I won't lie to you, *sarkar*. If I get work, I'll leave dacoity, but if not, then I'll go back to it but not in your state.'

'And if I ask you to forgo looting and pillaging all together, what will you do?'

'I would like to join the forces of the *sarkar*, where I can fight honourably and show my mettle better.'

'How many are there besides you in your group?' asked the rani next.

'There are about fifteen of us in the jungle, another sixty or sixty-five in the villages, and all my extended relatives.'

'What will they do?' asked the rani.

'They would also like to join your forces, *sarkar*.'

'And if I do not give them permission?'

'Then, except for the area under you, I will tell them to once again take to dacoity and pillaging.'

'Hmmm. And if I release you right now, where will you go?'

'Straight to Jhansi, *sarkar*.'

'What do you consider most holy?'

'Ganga ji, *sarkar's* feet, and then my sword, in that order.'

'Then, take the oath, Sagar Singh, and join my army,' said the rani.

'I accept, *sarkar*, but as an officer. Not as a sepoy,' replied Sagar Singh.

A smile lurked around the mouth of the queen, who liked the arrogance of this man, who was in shackles and bleeding but still defiant.

'Ok.'

Sagar Singh fell at her feet as there was a gasp from all who were present.

'Now I will return with you to Jhansi,' he declared.

'Not yet. Not till all your associates have also taken the oath and surrendered to me,' said the rani. 'If they do not do so, I will hunt them down and destroy them all.'

Sagar Singh looked at her loftily. 'I am their leader, *sarkar*. They follow me. They will all surrender and join your army.'

After that, they all settled down in the village. Sagar Singh's gang trickled in one by one, surrendered before the rani and took the oath. They all were recruited in the rani's army. Fifteen days after this incident, they all went back to Jhansi, leaving Sagar Singh to wait for further orders in his village.

Radhika had been fascinated by this dispensation of justice. The rani had by her wise decision turned a nasty situation to her own advantage. Radhika had heard that in the battles afterwards, Sagar Singh had died an honourable death, fighting on the battlefield. Of course, at this moment, he did not know this.

They all rode back to Jhansi and a message was sent to the residents at Cawnpore that the menace of Sagar Singh had been overcome. But it was not explained exactly how.

Chapter 16

News was reaching the people in Jhansi daily about clashes between the native soldiers and the white forces from various places. The rani was not happy. Radhika had read a lot about what a good military planner, strategist, and general the rani had been. But she also got first-hand experience of this very soon. They were still not fully prepared, and the rani knew that with half-baked preparations, victory was near impossible. Already, every day, clandestine meetings were being held to prepare Jhansi for the mutiny. Preparations to defend Jhansi were going ahead at full speed. Food and ammunition were being gathered, and the guns were being revived and repaired.

It was at this time when the ruler of Orchha, a widow like the Rani of Jhansi herself, but whose petition for the adoption of an heir had been granted, decided to attack Jhansi. At one time, Jhansi had been a part of Orchha, but later, it had been gifted to Samant Sarkar for his loyalty and became an independent state.

Radhika had, of course, seen many war films and imagined that what she had seen onscreen was actually what took place on ground. How mistaken she was! First and foremost, the beautiful, blood-stirring music that everyone was so used to hearing accompanying any war scene onscreen was replaced by so much ear-shattering sound that one could actually hear nothing. Sometimes, a person remained deaf for hours afterwards. Then, the plumes of dust and dirt were so thick that visibility was usually reduced to a few paces and it was impossible to see anything properly, leave alone focus and fire properly.

The first attack came when Nathe Khan, with a big army, attacked Jhansi along with the forces of Orchha. The queen of Orchha, Ladai Sarkar, declared that as at one time, Jhansi had been a vassal of Orchha, it should give up its independence and become its vassal once again. As the Jhansi forces were not yet fully ready for war, there was panic all around. A hasty meeting of all the senior ministers was called. Radhika was as usual standing behind the rani, along with the other ladies, and was surprised. Everyone else seemed to be panicking, but the rani was cool as a cucumber. She decided to lead her forces herself. She not only soothed down all the ruffled feathers but also gave responsibility to various people. Her only regret was that there had been little time to train more gunners. She gave responsibility for various gates of Jhansi to various senior gunners and then retired.

That night after dinner, the girls all gathered around her. '*Sarkar*, you promised to give us training as gunners also. I love to see the big guns firing,' declared Munder.

The rani smiled at her. 'In time, Munder, in time. I have every intention of training a complete battalion of women to take on the job of firing the big artillery guns. They can help the already trained gunners and learn from them and when required replace them too. I don't see any reason why women should lag behind men in such matters.'

There was a cheer from all the girls. Every woman present wanted to fire a big gun. The rani assigned five or six of them to assist the various gunners posted at strategic locations along the walls of the fort. Nathe

Khan's forces attacked Jhansi two days later. The battle with them lasted for two days and for the first time, the boom-boom of the big field artillery echoed in the air. Everything was engulfed in sulphur smoke and dust. There was no question of talking or even hearing orders. Sign language had to be resorted to in order to communicate. Many a time, a wall was breached, but the people of Jhansi were ready for this. Stone and mud, along with water and wood, had been gathered at various points and the breaches were immediately repaired. The men and women worked all night and sometimes even under fire to achieve this. The dust and the smoke were awful, and all of them coughed most of the time and ended up with totally black faces. Although the casualties were not heavy, many houses in the town caught fire and were destroyed. To Radhika's inexperienced eyes, the carnage seemed terrible.

When the first two or three artillery shells landed near Radhika, she nearly fainted, but after a time, she got used to the blasts. The dust and smoke nearly choked her, but they all stuck it out. This was Radhika's first experience of war. She had been attached to Ganga and another gunner at one of the important gates and now got first-hand experience of what it felt like to be under fire. It was not something that she really relished. It was full of noise and dust and the screams of the wounded. She had not seen so much blood and gore in her life till now. To say she was shaken a little was putting it mildly. And she remembered that in her time, in the two world wars, the carnage had been greater. How had they all managed to survive at all, she wondered. She also remembered her family and wondered what would happen if she got killed in this time zone. Would they miss her? How were they? Were they worrying about where she had disappeared to? Many a time, she found herself whimpering and wishing her mom was there and she could just hide her head in her lap.

The attack also affected little Damodar a lot. It was his first experience of a battle, and although he remained confined to the palace, the noise and the carnage were not hidden from him.

Every day, even while the fighting was going on, Radhika took to telling him a story from the journal she had found left behind by the British family. Damodar Rao found the stories fascinating. He suddenly turned very thoughtful. Every day, his ambition changed. One day, he wanted to become a pirate, the next day, it would be Robin Hood, and the third day, it would be someone else. The child loved to hear a different story every day.

The siege of Jhansi lasted for some time. The rani got impatient. Ladai Sarkar, the Rani of Orchha, was sending messages every day for Rani Laxmi Bai to surrender Jhansi. The rani got fed up and decided that enough was enough. One evening, after the evening meal, the rani called a conference of all her officers. It was decided that they would end the siege once and for all the next day. All night, frenzied preparation went on. Very early next morning, the gates of Jhansi Fort were opened and the call for battle was given. The Jhansi troops, led by the rani and her three lady generals, emerged and before the forces of Nathe Khan knew what had hit them, they had been decimated.

Nathe Khan's forces scattered like chaff in front of a stiff breeze and the forces from Jhansi made mincemeat out of them. They chased them for miles and wiped them out wherever they found them. Others surrendered while some just left their weapons and ran away. A triumphant Jhansi army returned to the fort amidst much fanfare.

Radhika had not taken part in this attack but watched it through field glasses from the ramparts. Most of the time, she could not see much, as the dust raised by the hooves of the horses covered everything. But she did manage to catch glimpses of the fierce fight going on between the two forces. She was impressed by the way the forces from Jhansi had handled themselves. They had been much smaller than the forces of Nathe Khan, but they had been more organised and each soldier, man or woman, had fought bravely.

Ladai Sarkar surrendered to Rani Laxmi Bai and went back to Orchha but pledged to support Rani Laxmi Bai in her struggle for freedom against the British rule.

Once the attack was over and things were back to normal, every day, after Radhika and the rani had finished their English lesson, Radhika would take the little boy to the park near the library and play with him there. Here, he usually brought his toys, which were mainly made of wood and mud, and his favourite game was battlefield. But after the attack, for a few days, he seemed to have lost his appetite to play the game. Before this, to Radhika's utter chagrin, he had always insisted that she play the British soldiers while he played the soldiers of Jhansi and insisted on winning. Now, he just sat and his toys lay around him. He also liked to draw and paint but he even refused to do these. Then, one day, while the two of them were sitting under a shady tree, he asked her a funny question. By now, he had taken to calling her *didi*.

'*Didi*, what if we lose a battle? Will mother and I have to leave Jhansi?'

Radhika did not want to answer that question because, unfortunately, she did know what had happened back in history. They all had read about the brave fight his adoptive mother had put up once she had left Jhansi and how she had finally died, but Radhika could not tell this to the child. It would be unfair. But Damodar was one persistent child and would not leave the topic. Finally, she mumbled, 'I suppose so.'

Damodar looked stricken. 'Then the *firangis* will come here!' he exclaimed.

'Yes, dear,' replied Radhika softly.

'Then, they will take all my toys!' said Damodar in distress.

'Well, perhaps some *firangi* child might play with them,' Radhika mumbled once more.

'I will never allow that!' Damodar almost shouted.

Radhika tried to calm him down, but he was very upset. He immediately picked up all his toys and looked fearfully around, as if expecting some white child to materialise and demand to take all his toys.

'I'll hide them,' he declared dramatically.

'Hide them?' asked Radhika, not comprehending. 'Hide them where?'

'Bury them under this tree so that when I return with mother, I can dig them out once more,' he declared, making Radhika smile. But he was serious. He ran and returned with a small spade and proceeded to dig a hole with the help of it.

'But you cannot put your toys directly into the hole dear. You must put them in a box of some sort,' said Radhika. 'Otherwise, they will disintegrate.'

Of course, there was no box to be found in the park. Suddenly, Damodar remembered that he had seen a beautiful box made out of some kind of metal that one of his old *ayahs* kept with her in which she kept her betelnuts and leaves.

'Come on, *didi*. We'll go and ask old Heera Mani for that box. I am sure she will give it to me,' he said, hopping up and down in excitement.

Radhika was not at all happy about this. She was sure the old retainer would give the yuvraj what he wanted, but would she be happy about it? Radhika tried to dissuade Damodar Rao as best as she could. 'Look, Damodar, it is not right to ask someone for something that belongs to them without compensating them for it,' said she.

'What is compensating?' he asked.

Radhika explained to him that it meant he must give the person something in return. Damodar sat down and thought about it for some time and then suddenly brightened up. 'I'll give her one of my toys,' he said and after that nothing would budge him from his stand.

After trying to change his mind to no avail, Radhika had to give in with a chuckle.

Damodar told Radhika that Heera Mani would be in the kitchen, and so to the kitchen they went looking for the old *ayah* of the yuvraj. The kitchen was huge and full of the most delightful smells. Various dishes were being cooked upon two or three fires. Two people were busy kneading flour to make *chapattis*. Two women were busy picking rice, which would be cooked for lunch. A delicious-smelling vegetable was being stirred in a huge *kadahi* by a man clad only in a *dhoti*. On another fire, a huge cauldron of *daal* was bubbling away merrily. Some women and young boys were busy chopping onions and other vegetables.

Heera Mani turned out to be a wizened old woman dressed all in white. She had been a widow since her childhood and had looked after Damodar before Radhika had come on the scene. As she was inordinately fond of chewing betelnut and leaves, she always carried a brass *paan-daan* with her. They found her sitting in the kitchen. She was putting betelnuts in betel leaves, along with cardamoms, some white paste, some rose paste, etc., wrapping up the leaves into tiny triangles, called *paan*, and offering the triangles to others even as she chewed one herself.

On seeing the two of them, everyone halted for a moment. Then, there was a cacophony of voices as they all gathered around and greeted them. It was obvious that they all loved the young yuvraj. Someone brought *sharbat* for the boy while someone else offered him a plate of *laddoos*. But Damodar was not interested in any of these at that moment. He marched straight up to Heera Mani and demanded, '*Mausi*, will you give me your *paan-daan*?'

'My *paan-daan*? What do you want with my *paan-daan*?' asked Heera Mani, looking astonished. 'I am sure your mother would be horrified to know that you have started eating *paan*!' she exclaimed.

'Of course not, *mausi*. I just want it for some work. I will give you this instead of it,' said Damodar and offered her the toy he had insisted on bringing with him. By now, everyone had gathered around and was listening and watching in puzzlement. Heera Mani looked at the little boy and suddenly gathered him up in her arms, her eyes welling up.

'You don't need to give me anything for the box, son. It is a privilege for me to give it to you,' she said and started emptying it out, sniffing and wiping her nose upon her *saree pallav*. By now, the solemn expression had vanished from the face of Damodar and his face was wreathed in a smile. He suddenly noticed the *sharbat* and the *laddoos*, and grabbing both, devoured them with the gusto only a young child can show. Very soon, Damodar and Radhika had the old brass *paan-daan* and they hurried back to the park.

In the park, Damodar wanted to put more things inside the box besides his toys. 'Let us ask Rani Maa for something,' he suggested.

'No dear. We should . . .' but Radhika never finished the sentence. Damodar was already off like a shot. Radhika took off after him after hiding the brass *paan-daan* behind a big bush. They found the rani sitting in what passed for the rani's office, where she was reading petitions made by various people.

'Rani Maa, Rani Maa!' yelled Damodar, bursting into the room breathlessly, with Radhika in hot pursuit.

The rani looked up from a petition and frowned. Then, seeing that it was her adopted son, she smiled. She immediately got up, picked him up, and hugged him.

'What's the matter, *beta*? What does my prince want?' she asked, kissing him.

'Rani Maa, give me something that I can put in my treasure chest,' demanded Damodar excitedly.

'Treasure chest?' asked the rani, raising her eyebrows.

'I and Radhika *didi* are going to bury my toys and a few other things so that no *firangi* gets hold of them if we are forced to leave Jhansi,' said Damodar simply. 'Whenever we return, I'll dig them out again, just like the pirates in the stories,' he told her. By now, Radhika had also halted and managed to get back her wind. The rani looked at her enquiringly.

Radhika looked uncomfortable but then explained what she and Damodar had been discussing.

'You must give me something of yours to bury alongside my toys,' insisted Damodar.

The rani was smiling by now. 'Actually, you need not worry, my prince. I have no intention of abandoning my Jhansi. I'll never give it up as long as I am alive. But still, if you insist, I'll give you a letter in my hand with my seal, saying that the contents of the box belong to my adopted son Damodar. What do you say to that?'

Damodar nodded reluctantly, not sure whether a letter would be such a great idea. Grown-ups could be very boring indeed. The rani put him down and sitting down once again, took out a quill and wrote upon a piece of stiff silk in English 'The contents of this box belong to my son, Damodar, and have been buried by him so that no *firangi* may get hold of them.' She waited for the writing to dry and then rolled the silk up and gave it solemnly to the little boy, who received it happily, reconciled to the eccentricities of grown-ups. Then, even as he turned, he grabbed one of the many quills lined up on the table to put in his treasure chest. These quills were special. They had the name of the rani engraved in gold upon them. They were for the exclusive use of the rani when she signed any letter or document.

Radhika and Damodar returned to the park happily. She picked up the *paan-daan* from behind the bush and after they had put in the letter from the rani along with her personal quill alongside the toys, they shut the box tightly. Then the two of them put the box inside the hole they had dug under the one and only small peepal tree in the park and spread the earth over it so that it was no longer visible. Finally, they sat back satisfied. Radhika looked at the solemn little boy and wanted to hug the little fellow and tell him that in case of a battle, no one would really be interested in his toys but did not have the heart to do so. He was so serious and apprehensive. After this, he insisted on making a rough map of the location of the buried box and hiding it inside a book in the library.

Radhika was surprised to find that she had begun to enjoy what she was doing along with the little fellow. It reminded her of her own childhood and gave her an odd thrill of sorts. That night, they only discussed the buried treasure before the yuvraj slept. Radhika gave him a kiss on the forehead once he had slept, before she went back to her own room. It had been a good day.

Chapter 17

Preparations in Jhansi were going on at top speed. This was the first time Radhika had seen a town prepare for a siege. Grain and dry rations of the lasting kind were gathered and stored in huge godowns. People had been found who could make explosives that gave off little smoke and were put to work. All the old artillery guns that had rusted because of not being in use were cleaned and made ready. Ammunition for them in the form of soft and hard shells was manufactured and stocked up in piles near them.

The rani held a meeting of the various heads of localities and gave them specific work, like looking after one specific gate or window in the fort and defending it. At the request of the women under her, she placed one or two of them under the charge of each artillery gunner, not only to help him in his work but also to learn from him so that they could relieve him for some time when required and manage the big guns themselves. It was a daring and unique concept in those days because female gunners were unheard of.

The *halwais* made tonnes of *shakarpare* and *laddoos*, along with *namakpare*, which would sustain the men and women during the siege without any time being wasted waiting for and eating cooked food, considering that it might or might not be possible to cook food during such an event. There was only one well inside the fort that supplied it with sweet drinking water. Three teams of Brahmins were given the task of drawing water from this well to supply it to the fighters and the others inside the fort. Each team would stay for eight hours and then rest while the next one took over.

Back in her own time, Radhika had read that the rani had been betrayed by one of her own men, a man who had pretended to be fighting for her but had actually been in the pay of the British. The man had been one of the gate keepers who had been manning a gun and had opened one of the gates for the British assaulters Unfortunately, she had forgotten the name of the man. Radhika tried her level best to try and remember the name of the double agent but to her utter chagrin failed to do so and it would not do just to give the rani a general warning. The rani would most likely call Radhika prejudiced and give her a lecture instead.

The rebellion had started prematurely in many places. In Jhansi, they were getting the news of various battles every day. The British were one by one putting down the rebellion in various places, taking over the key fortresses and towns and liberating the British in captivity there. The rani, of course, had by this time defeated Nathe Khan, who had been sent by Ladai Sarkar and had been making a nuisance of himself in western Jhansi. As for the town of Sagar, the army rebelled and looted it. There was rebellion in Jabalpur, and the flames of rebellion spread across the whole of Vindhyakhand.

In 1858, General Hugh Rose landed in Bombay with the full intention of taking revenge from the rebels. That same month, Delhi fell and the last Mughal emperor, Bahadur Shah Zafar, was taken prisoner. Two of his sons were taken prisoner and executed. Lucknow also fell. At

Cawnpore, Tatya Tope defeated at least three British generals. But the fall of Lucknow had a bad effect on the rebels. The populace in Awadh carried on the rebellion. The British carried out horribly cruel acts against innocent people in Allahabad and Fatehpur. All this news also reached Jhansi. Nana Saheb had lost the battle at Bithoor and barely managed to escape with his harem of wives and his stepmother to Lucknow. Rao Saheb and Tatya Tope came to Kalpi with their armies.

Through all this, Radhika never saw the rani turning a hair. She carried on her daily routine as if nothing was happening. Every Tuesday and Friday, she visited the *mandir* dedicated to Mahalakshmi. This was located upon the Lakshmi Taal, just outside Lakshmi Gate. Some days, she went in her *palki* and on other days on her horse. Sometimes, she used *purdah* in the town, and sometimes, she went without any *purdah*. Sometimes, she wore a *saree* and at others, she dressed like a man, in a *pyjama–kurta*. Sometimes, she went with an escort and at others totally alone. When she went in a *palki*, she was escorted by women decked out in silver jewellery, who ran alongside the *palki* in shoes made out of silk. A rider in front rode with an orange flag. In front of him were a hundred horse riders. Besides these, the *palki* was escorted by soldiers armed with weapons of war. After the *palki* came a contingent of Pathans, Mewaties, and Bundelkhandis. Besides her invariably rode Bhau Bakshi and some of her *sahelis*. She often took this opportunity to stop and to listen to petitions of the people while she was thus amongst them.

One day, her parade was going through the town when a poor Brahmin came and stood in front of her with folded hands. The parade halted. The rani asked Munder to find out what the man wanted. It turned out that the man had come from Banaras. His first wife had died. Now, no one was willing to give him their daughter because he was poor. They were asking him to arrange for four hundred rupees.

In those days, a new comptroller of the treasury had been appointed and his name was Ramchandra Deshmukh. The rani told Ganga to go and get him. When he came, the rani ordered him to take out four hundred rupees from the treasury and give it to the poor Brahmin. The Brahmin blessed her profusely. The rani smiled at him and said, 'Don't forget to invite me to your wedding.'

The Brahmin was so touched that he started crying. This story spread like wild fire all over Jhansi. People praised the largesse of the rani no end.

This was the time when the rani recruited many Muslims and Pathans into her service.

Winter was in the air. But battles were going on all over, and every day, they got news of such battles. In Bihar, Babu Kunwer Singh was fighting tirelessly at the age of eighty. They heard how when one of his arms got gangrenous, he chopped it off and kept up his fight. There was a story of one village in what is the present-day Uttar Pradesh, a village called Bodsar, in the district of Chandwak, in Jaunpur. Babu Kunwer Singh's daughter was married to a man in that village. The *sardars* of the village held a meeting to decide whether they wanted to join the rebellion or not. They were still debating over it when Babu Kunwer Singh's daughter sent in a *thali* of bangles and vermillion powder with the message that they should put on these bangles, like women, and stay at home as it was sad that while her eighty-year-old father fought for the freedom of the nation in Bihar, people here were still debating whether to join the rebellion or not. The people felt so ashamed that the village of Bodsar also finally joined the rebellion. Awadh was also up in arms.

General Hugh Rose was steadily advancing towards Jhansi. The British attacked many places simultaneously. Their theory that the day the leaders of the rebellion died, the rebellion would be over, was not really farfetched. The problem was that the Indian forces only answered to the man on top. If that leader got killed, they did not obey anyone else and tended to scatter, each for himself, and thus lost battles. There was no chain of command, as there was in the British ranks.

General Rose was approaching Jhansi from the side of the town of Sagar. Suddenly, one day, his troops were at the doorsteps of Jhansi and their pickets were visible from the battlements of Jhansi Fort. The gates of the fort were closed.

Chapter 18

The rani was everywhere. She supervised a lot of the preparations herself. She had recruited gunners and makers of explosives from all ranks and files, irrespective of their caste or creed. She wanted the best.

'I want enough stock so that we can withstand a siege of at least six months if required,' she had declared. As mentioned earlier, she had chosen men who could manufacture explosives that gave off no smoke or almost none so that the locations of the artillery guns were not revealed to the enemy by the smoke. She had recruited men who could mould metal guns that did not heat up readily and were ready for firing once again soon after they had fired once so that fewer guns would be required to defend any of the gates to Jhansi. Four guns would suffice where eight or ten would have been required earlier.

The rani decided to send a letter to Tatya Tope, who was at Kalpi, to come to her aid with his troops with the big guns at his disposal. She sent the letter with Juhi, one of the dancers working as secret service agents for the rani, and Ganga. The two women went off dressed in male attire to escape detection by the British.

General Huge Rose announced his arrival on the first day of the siege by firing a salvo over Jhansi Fort. The shell that landed in the town started the first fire, which was quickly brought under control.

On that day itself, the rani called all of her friends into her room. When they all gathered there, she called out to Munder, who entered with a tray on which were arranged small silken bags full of something.

'You all must be wondering why I have called you here tonight,' said the rani, smiling at them.

They all looked at her questioningly.

'I am presenting each one of you with a token of my appreciation for your loyalty and hard work. Each of these bags contains some gold coins. I am going to give each one of you one of these. Keep these with you. If things turn out badly and God forbid, we have to abandon Jhansi, then they might help you wherever you go.'

Kashi started crying. 'Why do you say that, Rani Sahiba? We will go with you wherever you go. You are our father, mother, everything.'

The rani looked at her enigmatically and smiled. 'I appreciate your sentiment, Kashi, but it just may not be possible. No one has any idea what the next few days hold for us. Fight, we will, to the best of our abilities. But what fate has in store for us is anyone's guess. I am just ensuring some security for each one of you, who has served me so diligently and faithfully.'

Then, she proceeded to give each one of them one bag, which she urged them to secret somewhere on their person. Radhika's little bag contained four gold sovereigns. Most of the girls were either crying or had wet eyes.

Once all the bags had been distributed, the rani looked at them all sternly. 'Now, I expect you all to give a good account of yourself against the British army in the coming days. Let them see that the women of Jhansi are at par with the men and are not behind them in anything.'

They all nodded in agreement and cheered loudly. Already, Radhika could feel a surge of excitement and enthusiasm flowing through her. If it had been possible, she would have ridden out of Jhansi and attacked the British encampment then and there. But she was not really prepared for the siege and the battle that followed in the next few days.

That very day, a message came from General Hugh Rose to the rani saying that as she was a British subject, she should open the gates of Jhansi and hand over the town to him. They would grant her a pension of five thousand rupees for life, on which she could retire wherever she chose to, outside Jhansi. Her personal jewellery would remain hers but she must hand over the treasury to the British, to whom it rightfully belonged.

The rani, with Radhika's help, sent back a letter saying, 'What about all my dependents? There are so many who are looked after totally by the grants from the treasury.'

The rude reply came that all this had to stop. No more pensions would be doled out. So would all the land attached to various religious places granted to them by the maharaja in his time be reclaimed and returned to the government. The religious places would once again become dependent upon donations of those who came for a *darshan*. Also, no more taxes would be paid into the maharani's treasury and all would go into the British treasury. The rani's dependents would no longer enjoy a pension from her treasury, as it would no longer belong to her.

The rani was furious. 'They want to make a beggar out of me. I will not allow that. *Main apni Jhansi kabhi nahin doongi*!' (I will never give my Jhansi) she declared.

'If you do not vacate Jhansi, then we will be forced to raze it to the ground,' threatened General Hugh Rose. The rani's reply was to fire a salvo of artillery shells into the British camp. And thus, the siege began.

Once again, the skies over Jhansi were rent by the sound of explosions and covered with dust and smoke. The shelling, which began every day early in the morning, ended only at night, when it became too dark for the gunners of both sides to see and aim fire accurately. The British tried to assault the fort twice but quickly realised that it was sheer suicide to do so. They withdrew and resumed shelling, trying to break the fortification.

Inside the fort, teams of men and women worked like trojans to repair any fortification that got breeched. The injured and the dead were quickly removed and others took their place. Food and water were supplied to the soldiers and gunners wherever they were on duty and in plenty so that they and their helpers did not have to leave their place for a drink or food. The men worked all day and the women took over at night. The British saw this through binoculars and were surprised and impressed at the women working as hard as the men at everything, from rebuilding damaged fortification to manning the guns, etc.

It was at one of the gates that Rao Dulhaju was stationed and with him was Munder. They worked side by side, and their grimy faces were testimony to the fact of how hard they were working. Munder told Rao Dulhaju to rest a little while she manned the gun as he looked tired. She respected the gunner a lot. Rao Dulhaju misunderstood her concern and made a pass at her. Munder was highly offended. That night, she complained to the rani about it.

'Bai Saheb, if I did not respect him as such a good gunner, I would have scratched his eyes out. What does he think I am? A whore?'

The rani was equally upset to hear this. But she advised Munder to keep her cool. 'Munder, as you rightly said, he is a very good gunner, and at the moment we need every gunner we can get. Swallow your pride and ignore him. I'll talk to him. But if even after this he makes a pass at you, you have my permission to beat him black and blue with your slippers.'

The rani called Rao Dulhaju and scolded him in front of everyone. 'These women respect the work you do, Rao Saheb, but that does not mean you can take them for granted and think they are cheap women. Don't make this mistake again.'

Rao Dulhaju tried to laugh off the whole matter. 'I was just trying to test her integrity, Rani Sahiba, and she misunderstood me. *Tauba! Tauba!* (God forbid!) I make a pass at her. I respect her too much for that,' he protested falsely. But inside, he was seething. The bitch had had the audacity to go and complain to the rani and had made him look small in front of all those stupid women. 'I could have kept her as my mistress just like that. But the

Rani Sahiba has given them too much importance, and it has gone to their heads. I feel like leaving and going home immediately. How dare they insult me like this!' thought Dulhaju.

Munder went back to work with a very sullen Rao Dulhaju. There were not enough gunners to make a replacement for her. The only thing the rani did was add Radhika to the group and asked her to help them out. It was her way of ensuring that Rao Dulhaju did not try any hanky-panky with Munder. Rao Dulhaju tried to appease Munder by saying, 'Bai ji, I meant no harm. I admire you ladies, who work as hard as us men.' But his words sounded hollow and false. The three of them worked side by side, not talking amongst themselves. It was not a very happy group. That day, somehow, Rao Dulhaju's gun did not function very well. His firing was erratic, and most of his shots landed either short of the encamped British soldiers or well beyond them. He also looked sullen and silent all day.

Chapter 19

When evening fell, Rao Dulhaju left his post to go home and rest a little. Munder took his place, with Radhika as her assistant. It was beside the point that neither of them had also left their post for most of the day and had been helping out, except for a few hours in the afternoon. After Rao Dulhaju left, Munder asked Radhika to go and fetch some food and water for the two of them. They would have their dinner at their post itself. There was no question of leaving it unattended.

It was already dark by the time Radhika scrambled down from the battlement. She was passing by a stinking old drain when she heard two men talking. She didn't know what made her halt, but one of them sounded like Pir Ali. The man had worked for one of the contenders for the throne of Jhansi but had turned and joined the forces of the rani. Somehow, Radhika had never trusted him. He was too smooth an operator. He was talking to another man. Radhika wondered who it was. Pir Ali was telling the other man, 'Today, once again I am going to the British camp for spying. It is a very dangerous mission. If I am caught, the British will shoot me like a wild pig. But why are you looking so glum, my friend?'

The other man snorted. Then he mumbled something Radhika could not catch, only catching the last part of his complaint. 'I felt so insulted. I have a good mind to just go home and never come back.'

'Don't do that, Rao Saheb.' Then, once again, there was some mumbling and then the second man was asking, 'Are you sure it is safe for me to come along with you? What if we are caught?' The first man reassured him, and the two men turned and entered the drain.

By now, Radhika's curiosity was raised. As far as she knew, Pir Ali had not been recruited as a spy by the rani. Why was he going to the British camp to spy, and who was the second man going with him? She decided to follow them.

The drain was stinking and slimy but high enough for Radhika to bend and walk. Very soon, she was out on the hillside and going towards the British encampment. The two men were mere shadows as they walked in front of her. They walked quite boldly, but Radhika had to be quite cautious. She did not want them to know that she was following them. As they reached the outskirts of the British camp, she heard the sentry on duty challenge them. Pir Ali gave the password, and they were immediately allowed to go into the camp. Something very fishy was afoot here thought the girl. She hid herself behind some bushes and waited.

The two men were inside the camp for quite some time. Then, they came out and started walking back towards Jhansi quite openly. They were talking between themselves.

'Rao Saheb, remember the signal of the red flag and what you have to do when you see it,' said Pir Ali.

'Of course, I remember,' declared the other man and they both entered the drain once again. Radhika followed after some time. She was still very puzzled. She had still not discovered who the other man was.

When Radhika at last reached Munder with food, Munder was quite annoyed as Radhika had taken so much time to fetch it.

'Did you stop to cook it, or did you fall asleep?' she asked sarcastically. Radhika apologised to her and related what she had seen and heard to her.

'There is something very shady going on here. Pir Ali gave the password, and he and the other man were allowed inside the British camp. I don't understand it,' she said.

'And what was it about a red flag? I think you should tell the Rani Sahiba,' said Munder.

Next morning, when they both went off duty and Rao Dulhaju was back on duty, they went to the rani and told her what Radhika had seen in the night. The rani was busy with a lot of things and did not really pay attention to them.

'Don't panic. Maybe Pir Ali has been recruited as a spy. I trust him. I don't have the details of everyone we use as a spy. And a red flag makes no sense. Maybe it is something akin to Moti Sai, the man the British felt we should hand over to them,' and she laughed.

In the beginning, the British had demanded that the rani hand over Moti Sai, the man supposedly in charge of the spy network of Jhansi, to them as one of the conditions for surrender. This had led to much mirth as there was no one by that name in Jhansi although they did have Moti Bai, the dancer, whose girls were doing a commendable job of spying against the British.

After that, the rani got busy with other administrative businesses and the information Radhika had handed over was put on the back burner. Radhika once again tried to recollect the name of the man who had betrayed the rani but could not remember for the life of her. She realised that it was vital that she remember as it might just turn the tide of the war, but she just could not. It was very frustrating. And unless she had some solid proof, the rani would not heed her advice. As it was, every day, they were losing good gunners to enemy shelling and they did not have adequate replacements. The female brigade was already stretched to the limit of its capability.

Meanwhile, the yuvraj, who had been in Radhika's charge for the past few months, had been returned to the charge of his old ayah and confined to the palace. The rani rightfully did not want him anywhere near where the firing was going on. But the sound of the thundering guns was even shaking the palace, and the child was not very happy about it. He missed his nightly story sessions with Radhika although the rani, in spite of her extra-busy schedule, made it a point to be there every evening to supervise his bedtime and to give him his dinner.

One morning, they heard that Tatya Tope was arriving with a massive army to help them. Everyone cheered up at this, and a current of hope went through the soldiers and also the ordinary people of Jhansi. Everyone tightened their belts and fought better that day. People kept waiting for Tatya's army to arrive and drive away the British attackers. One whole day passed and then another. On the third day, they all started feeling that it had just been a rumour. Then, on the fourth day, they got the tragic news that Tatya's army had arrived but unfortunately his heavy guns had sunk in the soft sand of the river while trying to cross it. His men had been trapped and massacred by the British, and he had had to give the order to retreat, leaving behind most of his guns. It was an ignoble defeat.

That day, Jhansi was shrouded in gloom. Everyone looked strained and was quiet. There was no cheer. They all knew that they had lost their one chance of any help and were now totally alone. Already, the stores of grains were running low. The rani had ordered the granaries of the palace to be opened to the public so that no one starved. But how long would they last, was the question.

Chapter 20

As mentioned earlier, throughout the siege, the rani had ordered that the yuvraj be confined to the palace. She did not want him to get injured or killed by an accidental explosion. Every time Radhika got a chance, she popped back in to look up upon him. The poor tyke was very brave. He did not like all the noise and dust and smoke but still insisted that he was ready to go out and fight the redcoats with his tiny sword.

On one particular day, all day long, the bombardment was relentless and heavy. There was no chance of repairing the damage to the walls of the fort. The day itself was depressing, with heavy clouds racing across the sky. It looked like it would pour at any moment. That would benefit Jhansi as there were not enough bucket brigades to douse out the fires started by the heavy bombardment and the town was blazing under the heavy shelling.

Munder was manning a gun that was located on top of Orchha Gate and Radhika was helping her. They had already beaten back two assaults by the redcoats. Rao Dulhaju's guns once again seemed to be misfiring as their shells landed anywhere except upon the enemy, and he was still in a sullen mood. After trying to get back into Munder's good books by apologising, he had not addressed a word to either of them, realising that his insincerity was apparent.

Suddenly, Radhika saw what looked like a red flag raised from behind a low hillock behind which the redcoats had deployed themselves. She was wondering if this was what the two men that night had been talking about when she saw Rao Dulhaju leave his gun and jump down and run towards the gate. The gate was a heavy one and locked with a heavy padlock. But Dulhaju carried an iron rod. Before they realised what he was up to, he had rammed it behind the lock and broken the lock.

Munder saw this and immediately understood what he was up to. She fired her gun for the last time, drew her sword, jumped down from the gate, and raced after Dulhaju, shouting out to Radhika to run to the rani and tell her she had been betrayed and the gates had been opened. Radhika saw Munder pounce upon Dulhaju, who had pulled open the heavy gates, and shouting, 'You traitor!' she killed him with one stroke of her sword.

Munder leaped forward and tried to shut the gate once again, but it was too heavy for her. By now, the British soldiers had come out from behind the small hillock and rushing to the gate, were pushing at it with all their might. They managed to open the gate completely and surrounded Munder, whose last words to Radhika were, 'Go, Radhika! Tell the rani she has been betrayed,' before she went down fighting.

Radhika did not wait to see more. Her heart pounding, she turned and jumping upon her horse, which was tethered nearby, raced through the streets towards the palace, where the rani would be resting or at her prayers at that time. There was no time for her to even feel sick at this betrayal.

At the palace, the rani had just finished her evening prayers and was dressing to go out and look at all the *bandobast*. A few of her lady soldiers were with her.

Jhalkari was also there. Radhika dashed into the rani's presence and without any preamble blurted out all that she had seen.

'Rani Sahiba, the red flag I had mentioned that day was a signal from the redcoats. They showed it today just at sundown, and Rao Dulhaju opened the gates and now the British have entered the town. Munder is fighting them, but she is outnumbered,' she gasped, out of breath.

The rani looked at her, aghast and then in despair as the ramifications of this betrayal quickly became clear.

'You must get out with the yuvraj, Rani Sahiba. The British should not catch you,' said Jhalkari.

'But they are bound to give chase,' said the rani, looking sick, her thoughts for her Jhansi and its people.

'Not if you are seen to be going out in the opposite direction,' said Jhalkari shrewdly.

The rani looked a little confused. 'What do you mean, Jhalkari?' she asked.

'Rani Sahiba, you go out through Bhandari Gate towards Kalpi. I will take a contingent of our *nari sena* and wearing your clothes go straight towards the British camp and declare that I am the rani and am surrendering to them. By the time they find out I am not you, you will have gone far,' and Jhalkari laughed.

'But when they realise you are not me, they will kill you,' said the rani in distress.

'So what? To die for you has always been my ambition. Please give me the honour of doing this,' said Jhalkari humbly.

The rani protested, reluctant to leave Jhansi at the mercy of the redcoats, but all the other women present sided with Jhalkari. Someone immediately brought some of the rani's clothes for Jhalkari. When they brought some of the jewels, Jhalkari refused. 'My own are more than enough to confuse them,' she declared.

Two groups were formed. Radhika was attached to Jhalkari's group so that there would be someone who would be able to talk to the British. The yuvraj was also brought. Everyone gathered in a little courtyard. The horses were brought there and everyone mounted them. Radhika gave the yuvraj a hug and whispered to him, 'Be brave and look after your mother.' The yuvraj nodded solemnly. The rani tied the yuvraj to her back with a shawl. Darkness had fallen, but the various fires started in the town by the bombardment lit up everything in a grisly way. This courtyard gave out directly onto the streets of Jhansi, and very soon, the two groups were riding through the streets of Jhansi in two different directions.

By now, the fighting had spilled over onto the streets. The people of Jhansi were fighting for all they were worth, with everything they had, be it crowbars, swords, or just sticks and even pans. Jhalkari's group was near the *pilkhana*, that is, a *haathi-khana*, when it met a large group of mounted redcoats, who immediately attacked them. Everyone drew swords, and there was a real free for all. Even Radhika had been equipped with a sword, but within the first few minutes, someone had hit her sword hand hard and it had fallen. The next moment, she toppled over and tried to save herself but fell badly on her back. She managed to roll quickly to the side.

Otherwise, she would have been trampled by the horses. She managed to roll into the *pilkhana* and lay there in the dark, her heart in her mouth, sweat beading her forehead, hoping no one had seen her and no one would come after her. The fighting, which was fierce, ended as swiftly as it had started. Radhika held on to her breath as she heard some riders riding away. When things became quiet, she picked up the courage to peep out and saw that the street was littered with the corpses of the redcoats. So, the horses going away had belonged to Jhalkari's group. Radhika was glad that they had got away. Then, it struck her. She had been left behind! What was she going to do now?

Chapter 21

Radhika peeped out, and although it was night, the streets were lit up by the various buildings that had been set on fire. She saw some soldiers fighting the local people in the street at a little distance. Then, a group of women suddenly materialised out of a door, carrying pots and pans of various sizes, and on reaching the group of fighting soldiers, began hitting them with these right, left, and centre. They seemed not bothered that the redcoats were armed with swords. They were just out to help their men folk in any way possible. In fact, the people fought so ferociously that the redcoats, realising they were outnumbered, turned and came thundering towards the *pilkhana*. Radhika shrank back into the shadows, but the racing horsemen had no time or inclination to see or challenge anyone. They just thundered past and disappeared down the narrow lane into the night.

Radhika was still rooted to the spot, petrified, when the group of civilians who had attacked the redcoats gave a cheer and moved off in the other direction. Once again, the narrow lane became deserted. Radhika sat back on the ground and wondered what she should do.

She was still sitting in a bemused state, totally undecided, when something soft touched her shoulder. She turned around and gave a scream and nearly jumped out of her skin. A huge shadow was looming over her. Then, she realised that it was an elephant. After all, she was in the *pilkhana*. The poor animal had been left behind.

Obviously, it was a tame one and the poor thing was also very scared. It kept caressing Radhika's arm with its trunk. She patted it helplessly.

'Oh, you poor thing! I know. You must be scared. But so am I. Your *mahauts* seem to have abandoned you. Poor you! I am also stranded. What are we to do now?' She asked, as she stood up.

Just then, there were heavy footsteps on the street outside the entrance of the *pilkhana*. Someone was coming! Radhika quickly rolled into the shadows towards the back of the *pilkhana*. She could feel her heckles rising. It could be anyone. She stood up with her back to the wall and looked desperately around for a weapon of any kind. Her sword had vanished in all the fighting earlier. There was nothing that she could see that she could use as a weapon to defend herself with. Then, she sensed something move against her back. A stone in the wall was loose. She felt behind and found it. She quickly pulled it out and held it firmly in her hand, ready to defend herself if required.

The footsteps halted outside the *pilkhana*. A shadow entered. As the person was silhouetted in the little light at the entrance, Radhika saw that it was a man who carried two heavy sacks upon his back. The man put down the sacks and then turned to look around. He immediately spotted the elephant and went over to it and caressed its trunk. He talked in a low tone to the distressed creature and then went to a corner and returned with a *howdah*. He made the elephant kneel down and tied the *howdah* upon its back. Then, putting the sacks in the *howdah*, he climbed in himself and then went out with the elephant.

Once again, Radhika was alone. She came out to peep out of the entrance. She was just beginning to think that maybe she could make her way back to the palace when another group of people came thundering down the lane and made her dart back into the shadows. As they went by, she took a breath of relief and then realised that this time she had darted towards another side of the *pilkhana* and here there was no wall. In the dim light coming from outside, she saw a gaping hole. There seemed to be some kind of passage or tunnel leading out of the *pilkhana*. Suddenly she thought that may be it was a branch of the secret passage from the room occupied by the yuvraj, the branch the soldier had mentioned.

Outside, Radhika suddenly heard the ominous roll of thunder as without warning, black clouds rolled across the heavens, cutting out all light. She remembered the tiny torch that she had had the sense to always keep with her, ever since the rani had told them that they might have to abandon Jhansi. She showed the torch around. The passage led from around a big rock set in the wall of the *pilkhana*. She had somehow managed to dart right into its mouth from the other side. If you stood at the door of the *pilkhana*, you would probably not be able to see the passage.

Radhika suddenly heard another set of footsteps coming towards the *pilkhana*. Outside, thunder and lightning were lighting up the sky. She quickly darted into the passage and started running up the tunnel. The man who had entered the *pilkhana* now apparently knew about the passage, because she heard him enter it and then, probably hearing her footsteps, he started following her. Panic rose up inside her, and she started running. The man behind also started running. Already, Radhika could hear the thunder and lightning outside fading, as the two of them got deeper inside the tunnel. She kept peering over her shoulder but could not make out much in the dark corridor, but she could hear the man behind panting. Images of someone with a sword trying to cut her up were making her feel dizzy. She was breathless and tears were flowing down her face. Just when she thought she would collapse, there was a huge sound of thunder. And there, a few yards away, a glow started lighting up the walls of the passage.

Radhika stopped, winded. A sob broke from her. Even as she watched, the glow transformed itself into the lift. She could not believe her eyes! There was her beloved lift, the one in which she had come into this time warp, and there it stood, waiting for her.

The man chasing her had also halted. Then, he swore and started towards Radhika again. He was coming nearer and was about to catch her. She didn't know where the strength or energy came from, but she made a final dash towards the lift. As she approached, its doors opened and she fell into it. She could hear the man behind cussing and calling her all sorts of filthy names, but she managed to jump up and push the button for closing the door and to activate the lift. The last thing she heard was the frustrated shout of her chaser, and then there was complete darkness.

Chapter 22

Radhika must have passed out in the lift, because for how long she lay completely oblivious to everything she had no idea. As she came to, she realised that she was soaking wet and shivering and that the lift was standing still upon the landing of her room. She struggled to sit up and somehow managed to open the latch and get out onto the tiny balcony. Thankfully, she found that the door to her room was unbolted. She almost fell into her room and just stripping off her soaking clothes got into her pyjamas, which surprisingly were still upon her bed. Then she fell into her bed and passed out.

Radhika didn't know how long she slept, but when she opened her eyes and found herself back in her room, she looked around in disbelief. The happenings of the last six or seven months flashed before her eyes. Had she been dreaming everything? Then, she saw the soaking, dirty dress that she had discarded upon the floor the night before. She scrambled out of her bed and as she picked up the dress, a little silken bag fell out of it and onto the floor with a clink. She quickly picked it up and opened it to find the four gold sovereigns the rani had presented her inside it. Confused and stunned, she slumped back upon her bed, wondering what had happened. She had obviously been in Jhansi, with the rani, around 1857, but then why was everything just as she had left it so many months back? Had her parents and grandmother kept a shrine for her? She was really touched.

Just then, she heard her mother calling out, 'Hey, lazybones. How long do you intend sleeping in? So what if it is a Sunday? Brunch will be ready in half an hour.'

Radhika was even more confused. It had been Saturday evening when the freak storm had hit the lift. She got off the bed once again and padded over to where her cell phone lay upon her study table. Her gaze fell upon the date. It showed the 4th of July. She shook her head and looked once again. But how could that be? The day she had left had been the 3rd of July and she had been away for so many months. But apparently, barely a few hours had passed here. Just then, she heard someone approaching her door.

Radhika instinctively grabbed the crumpled and dirty dress and bundled it out of sight into her cupboard, just managing to jump back into bed and pretending to be asleep when her mother knocked and walked into her room.

'Hey, lazybones. Your favourite *chhole bhature* is on the menu for brunch today. Hurry up and dress and come down. You know how Daadi Maa hates anyone to be late. It is nearly eleven, you know.'

'Oh no!' exclaimed Radhika. She could not believe it! Daadi Maa really would throw a fit if any of them was late for a meal. She jumped out of bed and dived into the bathroom. She broke the record for a bath and her morning ablutions. It was while she was bathing that she realised that her hair had grown longer and her complexion had become darker. She wondered how she would explain these to her family. After her bath, she scrunched her hair into a ponytail and only hoped no one would notice the change in her appearance. She was yet undecided what she exactly wanted to tell them and how much. Even they, who indulged her so much, may think she was pulling a stunt of some sort and laugh at her. She lathered some cream onto her face and smothered a base upon it, hoping to conceal the tan. Finally, scrambling into the first outfit she could lay her hands on, she reached the dining room just a second before Daadi Maa and thankfully slid into her chair. The brat was already there, and so was her mother.

The brunch went off peacefully, and Radhika ate silently, still struggling to come to terms with the fact that she was back in her own time. The only one who seemed to notice something was not the same was Daadi Maa, who kept giving her speculative looks but refrained from saying anything.

After brunch, Radhika went out to the lift and thoroughly inspected it. But there was nothing the matter with it. There it was, as solid as ever. Taking a deep breath and steeling herself, she stepped into it, not sure if she would be again thrown back into 1857. Then, muttering a little prayer, her heart hammering, she pressed the button to go down. The lift went down smoothly, and she remained solidly in current-day Noida. Once down, she pressed the button to go up and the lift slid up, conveying her safely to the little balcony outside her room. Radhika heaved a sigh of relief. But the brat heard her going up and down and came into her room to find out what she was up to.

'What are you doing? Why are you going up and down in the lift?' he asked her suspiciously.

'None of your business!' she retorted. There was no way she was going to tell him about all that she had experienced. He would laugh his head off. As it was, he was looking at her as if she had gone mad. By now, Radhika was feeling that maybe she had gone mad and dreamt everything. But what about the dirty dress in her cupboard? From where had that come? And what about the gold coins in that little silk bag? They were as real as could be. She was thoroughly confused.

Just to ensure that all was ok, she went up and down in the lift a number of times. Finally, the brat got bored of this apparently aimless activity and went away, making a gesture indicating that she had gone bonkers.

Radhika decided to give the dirty dress to Moonshine Drycleaners, who were located in the small market nearby. She knew that if she tried to wash it at home, there would be too many questions asked that she would not be able to answer. So, she smuggled it out in a plastic bag and gave it to be drycleaned.

Chapter 23

In the next few weeks, Radhika found that she was missing the new friends she had made in Jhansi. She specially missed the yuvraj. She had read up upon the Rani of Jhansi and felt sad that she had not been able to do much to save her in spite of knowing what the future held for her. But despite trying, she could not go back in time again. It was very frustrating for her!

It was a few weeks later. One evening, they had just finished listening to the nine o'clock news on Doordarshan. Daadi Maa insisted that everyone listen to it, however boring the youngsters found it. Once the news was over, the brat wanted to change the channel, but before he could do so, Radhika saw that a debate had been announced between two historians who had been doing research on the Battle of 1857. She snatched the remote from him and in spite of his protests refused to let him change the channel. Two eminent historians had been invited to talk about the great Rani of Jhansi. Very recently, some letters written in English had come to light. The rani was supposed to have penned them herself. But there was a big doubt about it. One of the historians was the Dr. Dastoor who had officiated at the seminar held on the Rani of Jhansi at the university and even now was sure the rani knew no English.

'Of course, she knew English!' exclaimed Radhika, without thinking.

'How do you know?' challenged the brat immediately. 'She never learnt English.'

'She . . .' began Radhika and then shut her mouth. How was she to tell them that the rani had learnt English from a European lady and then from Radhika herself. Maybe there was no historical account of that anywhere.

'*Beta*, in those days, ladies especially did not learn English. They believed that it would compromise their *dharam*,' said Daadi Maa.

'But the rani was very progressive. She believed in gender equality!' protested Radhika.

'How do you know? You are talking as if you knew her,' snorted the brat.

'Well . . . in those times she raised an all-women army, didn't she!' retorted Radhika. 'Right, Daadi Maa? And there were female generals commanding her army. She only looked at the ability of a person not at their gender,' said Radhika.

'She was an exception. And I am proud of the fact that one of my ancestors served right under her,' said Daadi Maa. The brat made a face, while Mrs. Rai junior tried to supress a smile.

On the show, the two experts were still going on and on. One of them mentioned some gold *mohars* that had also come to light recently. They had been found with a family where they had been handed down from one generation to another. The family had been claiming that the rani had given these *mohars* to one of their ancestors who had been with her during the rebellion. Radhika remembered the gold *mohars* hidden in her cupboard. She decided it would not be a bad idea to get one of those authenticated by the expert.

'Daadi Maa, after reading your journal, I thought I would show it to one of these experts. Will you let me do that, Daadi Maa? Please! It may turn out to be valuable. You never know,' pleaded Radhika.

'Of course, it is valuable, but you must be careful that they don't damage it,' said Daadi Maa.

'Oh, thank you! Thank you, Daadi Maa!' and getting up, Radhika danced over to her and gave her a big hug.

'Oh, go along with you!' said Daadi Maa gruffly, but Radhika could see that she was pleased. The brat was frowning and Mrs. Rai junior looked a little unsure but resigned. So, it was arranged. Radhika would find out the address of the professor and pay him a visit. She was over the moon with excitement.

Chapter 24

The next day, Radhika, decided to visit the National Archives, located at the intersection of Janpath and Kartavya Path (the government had recently renamed Rajpath as Kartavya Path). She thought she would do some research before she approached the professors who had been interviewed. She just might find some mention of what she had experienced.

'Where are you going today?' asked her mother at the breakfast table.

'I want to do a bit of research in the National Archives for a paper I am writing,' said Radhika glibly.

'Oh, I also did some research there during my college days,' said her mother.

'Really, Mom. What is it like?' asked Radhika.

'Well . . . not too good,' said her mother.

'What do you mean by that?' asked Radhika, her ears all alert now.

'Well . . . it was an experience,' said her mother.

'The National Archives were musty and followed a system where their content was listed upon a card index system. One had to browse through this card index system for hours before one could fine anything. The people there were not very helpful either. The old ledgers and books and halls were so full of dust that you had to tie a mask before you entered them.

'The lady at the reception that day was also exceptionally rude.

'So, I suggest you carry some dusting cloths and a mask. Otherwise, you might find it difficult. And do carry some sort of identity papers, like your ID card, or they will not let you enter.

Radhika nodded and taking a few old rags and a mask, she set off for the National Archives. At last, she could go through the journals. Her heart was beating hard. What would she find in them, she wondered.

The National Archives turned out to be a far cry from what her mother had described. Of course, she had to get a temporary pass made in a small office at the entrance, but she faced no difficulty in getting the pass. The people there were very helpful. When she told them that she wanted to do research on Jhansi ki Rani, one of them suggested that she refer to the Abhilekh Patal. This was a search portal providing access to all the old documents in the archives, an initiative of the NAI to make its rich treasure of Indian archival records available to one and all at the click of a button. On this portal, old documents were being converted into microfilms that she could get access to without handling the actual fragile originals.

The hall Radhika was directed to was filled with people, presumably scholars, all sitting at neat, clean desks with computer screens in front of them upon which the digitalised documents they had requested, if available, were displayed for them to read. There were a few huge gurneys with thick tomes upon them, but they were very few. Everything seemed to have been streamlined and as for dust, there was hardly any to speak about. Radhika was glad no one had searched her bag. They would have wondered why she was carrying rags with her. As for making copies, she just had to put in an application with a request and the copies were made for her and given to her for a nominal fee. The entire ambience had changed, and Radhika was happily surprised.

Radhika located the journals she wanted to go through. They were at first disappointing. Mostly, they were a chronical of who had gone on leave and who had returned, how much pay had been disbursed to whom by the chancery in Jhansi, and so on. She found out that most people had got paid two *annas* or four *annas* but a few had received the princely sum of a rupee or two. Near the end of the ledger, she came across a section where there were petitions attached for grants of money. People had requested the British to grant them money for the marriages of their daughters or for some other religious ceremony. Radhika had started feeling that she was wasting her time. And then, suddenly, she saw it. At first, it did not register, then it hit her. It was a letter written in English. It had faded with time but was still legible. At the bottom, it had been signed by Rani Laxmi Bai and there was the official seal of Jhansi upon it. It was a request for the release of one lakh rupees for the thread ceremony of Damodar Rao from the funds held by the East India Company in trust for him. The rani had written this letter to the British resident. Radhika remembered it clearly because the rani had not written this letter herself. In fact, Radhika had written it for her and the rani had signed and stamped it with her seal. Radhika looked at the letter carefully. There was no doubt. It was the letter she had written. She got goosebumps.

She now knew that she had not imagined her adventure. She had gone back in time to 1857 and had met the Rani of Jhansi and interacted with her. She requested and got a photocopy of the letter. Now, all she had to do was to get someone to authenticate the gold *mohars* that she had brought back with her from that time.

Chapter 25

The next day, after her classes were over, Radhika made her way over to the Department of History. Dr. Dastoor was the head of the department. When Sunny wanted to know why she was not catching the bus with him, she made a lame excuse about wanting to meet an old friend from one of her old schools whom she had spotted and found where she was staying. 'Do tell Daadi Maa and Mom I'll be back an hour later than usual,' she told him. Sunny looked at her a little puzzled and then deciding that if she did not want to introduce him to her old friend, that was her business, he shrugged and went off.

Radhika watched him walking away and realised why he had given her that enquiring look, but she had not yet told him about her adventure in the lift, lest he laugh at her. She had decided she would tell him everything once she herself was sure of what had happened to her. She carried the precious sovereigns in the silk purse that the rani had given her safely tucked into her purse. She had made an appointment with Dr. Dastoor for three o'clock in the afternoon.

The Department of History turned out to be a dusty affair, tucked into one corner of the Arts Faculty. Classes were over for the day and the classrooms closed, but the office of the head was open. The corridor outside was deserted. Radhika felt a little nervous as she knocked upon the door. A gruff voice bade her enter.

Dr. Dastoor looked at her from behind thick soda glasses. His office was dusty, and he himself looked rather dusty. He was busy working on a computer upon his desk. He looked annoyed at being interrupted.

'Yes?' he enquired, looking impatiently at Radhika.

Radhika introduced herself, and he frowned at her. Clearly, he had forgotten about the appointment. Then, rather reluctantly, he waved her to a chair that seemed not to have been wiped in some considerable time. Radhika had the greatest desire to take out her hanky and wipe it before she sat down upon it but decided against it as it would have been rather insulting.

'Now. What can I do for you?' asked Dr. Dastoor.

Radhika pulled out the silk purse and taking out the sovereigns placed them before him. He looked at them and then asked, 'What are these? And where did you get them?'

Radhika did not want to tell him the truth about her adventure in time travel. So, she told him a cock-and-bull story about discovering the coins amongst some things in an old box that had been passed down through the generations in her family. She asked him if he could help her in authenticating them. He opened a drawer and taking out a magnifying glass proceeded to examine them through it. Radhika could see the excitement building up in his face.

'Tell me once again where you found them? Have you any more of them?' he asked with suppressed excitement.

Radhika repeated her story. 'I found them amongst my late grandmother's things. I believe they were given to her by her own grandmother,' she lied glibly, silently apologising to Daadi Maa for making her "late", i.e. dead, while she was still hale and hearty.

'Why don't you leave these with me? I would like to show them to a colleague or two and get their opinion before I commit myself,' said the professor.

This was something Radhika was not prepared for. She didn't know what exactly she had thought he would do. She had had a vague idea that he would just examine them and tell her. How foolish she had been! Of course, he would like to consult some more experts upon it, find out how she came to possess them, etc. She could have kicked herself for being so naive! But she had little option. Now that he had seen them, she would have to leave them with him.

He saw the reluctance upon her face and gave her a horrible tobacco-stained smile. 'Don't worry. I'll keep them safely. You can return after a week, and then I'll be able to tell you what you want to know,' and he patted her hand, making Radhika cringe. He had bony hands, which looked more like a skeleton's hand with a glove upon it than anything else.

Radhika had no choice. Leaving them with him reluctantly, she went back. It was two days later when she opened the newspaper that a prominent bit of news leaped out at her from the front page.

'Indian Archaeologist Discovers Golden Sovereigns Minted in 1845.'

It was followed by how Dr. Dastoor, the head of the Department of History at Delhi University, had discovered the coins amongst a collection of some old coins he had found in a trunk belonging to his grandmother.

Radhika could not believe it! The man had not only stolen her sovereigns but also stolen her story. She was furious. She immediately tried to ring him up on her cell phone. It rang and rang and rang, and then he picked it up and immediately cut it. Of all the cheap tricks! After that, for the next few hours, his cell phone was switched off. Radhika decided to go to the university and confront the man. She reached the university, only to find that Dr. Dastoor had gone off on long leave. The people in the department gave her his address. She rushed over to the house, which was located in a good locality, and rang the bell. The door was opened by a sleezy looking lady dressed in a sloppy housecoat.

'Yes?' she frowned at Radhika.

'Is Dr. Dastoor at home?' asked Radhika.

'No,' replied the woman abruptly and was about to shut the door in Radhika's face when Radhika put her foot in it.

'Where has he gone? I have to see him. It is urgent,' she said hastily.

The woman scowled at her. 'I don't know where he has gone. He never bothers to tell me.'

'When will he be back?' asked Radhika, desperate by now.

'Why do you want to know?' demanded the woman belligerently. By now, she was looking suspiciously at Radhika.

'He has something of mine that he was supposed to have returned today. It is important,' Radhika blurted out.

For a moment, the expression on the woman's face softened.

'Listen, if it is a thesis or a research paper of yours, you can kiss it good bye. By the time he returns from wherever he has gone off to, his publisher would have already published it under his name. And you will not be able to do anything about it. So, now, just go. It is already too late,' and she shut the door in Radhika's face.

Radhika slowly walked back and was still reeling from the shock of finding that the professor had stolen her evidence when she found herself standing in front of the university café. She was truly shaken up. Now, she had no evidence left of her time travel. What was she going to do? She decided to have a cup of tea while she tried to sort out what had happened before she went home. She needed the tea badly.

Five minutes later, she was sipping the hot, oversweet brew when someone tapped her on the shoulder.

'What crime has the poor tea committed, Rats?' calling her by the nickname he had given her. 'Why this terrible scowl, as if you are drinking poison and not just tea?' asked Sunny, plonking himself next to her. Radhika glowered at him, and immediately Sunny put up his hands in mock defence.

'Hey, I haven't said or done anything to offend you, girl. What's wrong?'

Radhika gave a reluctant smile. 'Nothing and everything.'

'And what do you exactly mean by that?' asked Sunny, looking puzzled. 'Wait. Let me get a cold drink, and then you can tell me.'

'It is nothing that I can tell you,' declared Radhika, looking lost.

'Oh, come on! What are friends for? Hold your horses for just two minutes,' admonished Sunny and went off to get a cold drink for himself.

Radhika was still unsure but then decided rather reluctantly that it was probably time she confided in someone whom she could trust. Once he was back, over the next half an hour, Radhika told him all about her adventure in time travel and then how the wily professor had stolen her evidence and passed it off as his own find.

Sunny heard her through, without speaking a word, looking stunned at her description of her interaction with the rani and the others. Radhika had thought he would scoff at her, but once she had finished, he only looked furious.

'You know, I have heard of such things but never believed in them before. If it had been any one excepting you, I would have thought they were trying to make a fool out of me. What a rotten rascal! Just let him return. I and some of my friends will do his *kambal* parade.'

That made Radhika smile. That was such a typical *fauji* expression. It meant putting a blanket over the potential victim, ensuring that his face is covered so that he is not be able to identify his attackers, and then proceeding to bash him up.

'Anyway. I am already feeling better,' declared Radhika. 'But still, it does not really solve my problem. How do I prove what happened to me?'

The two friends sat in silence for some time, and then Radhika shook herself up. 'Forget about my problem for the time being. I dare say, we'll find a solution to it in time. What about you? Haven't seen you for a while.'

'Oh, things are not going too well for me too,' said Sunny gloomily.

'Why? What has happened?'

'I am to go with grandmother during the Dusshera holidays,' said Sunny, sounding most unhappy.

'Going? Where?' asked Radhika .

'To Babina. Grandfather's former regiment is located there at present. Every year, they invite grandma to their raising day. This year, she wants me to escort her. It will be such a bore,' he blurted out.

'Oh!' said Radhika. Then she looked at him softly. 'Come on. She is an old lady and probably is afraid to travel alone now,' said Radhika, patting his hand. 'By the way, where is Babina?'

'It is the cantonment for Jhansi,' said Sunny, still looking gloomy. 'What will I do amongst all the officers and oldies?' he protested. Then he looked contrite. 'But I suppose I'll have to go. She loves to go every year. It is the one holiday she loves to indulge in. I suppose I can stand the boredom for the four days,' he ended, sounding resigned.

'Come on. It can't be so bad. If I know the army, you will have a lot of entertainment. Papa's regiment had their raising day, and everyone nearly went mad for a whole week, partying and partying and celebrating. There were competitions, and even a *pagal* gymkhana.' said Radhika, looking a little nostalgic.

'But what will I do with all the oldies?' grumbled Sunny. 'Most of the officers attending either have children who are too young or they themselves belonged to the regiment at one time. I will feel like a fish out of water.'

Radhika laughed. 'Stop grumbling, you dope. Try and enjoy yourself. I wish I could have accompanied you,' she said wistfully.

'I know,' said Sunny grumpily.

The two friends finished their tea and then headed for home in the bus. Though still feeling down in the dumps, having shared their problems, they were both in a better frame of mind than before.

Chapter 26

Radhika reached home, to find her mother and grandmother deep in an argument.

'I can go on my own, *bahu*. Why should you deprive yourself and the children of the Dusshera holidays? As it is, only my presence is needed at the moment.'

'No, *maa ji*. You cannot go alone. This running around courts alone at your age, not done,' protested the junior Mrs. Rai.

'Well, as I said, my friend Bhanumati will be going there with her grandson for the raising day of her late husband's regiment. I am sure I can go in the train with them. Once there, my cousin and his family will surely look after me,' declared Daadi Maa.

'Where is Daadi Maa going?' asked Radhika, throwing her purse and bag down upon a chair and plonking herself on a sofa.

'Oh, my cousins, who is nearly eighty-five and has been living in the ancestral *haveli* at Jhansi, is now going to live with his son in Canada. He has suggested selling the old *haveli* as it is falling apart and not worth repairing. As you know, your great-grandfather – my father – were four brothers. They each had one child only. The only child of the eldest brother is settled in Australia. The one living in Jhansi is the son of the second brother. My father was the third brother, and I am his only child. The son of the youngest brother is no more but has left behind two children, who are both claimants to the *haveli*. Now my cousin wants all of us to gather at Jhansi so that the *haveli* can be sold and the money shared amongst all of us. But before being sold, the *haveli* has to be put on all our names. For that, we all have to appear in court in front of a judge,' explained Daadi Maa. 'Since everyone is gathering there during the Dusshera holidays, I proposed that I too will go there at that time while you all visited your father so the paper work can be done, but your Mom thinks I cannot go alone. *Bahu*, I am still not so old and infirm as you think,' protested Daadi Maa, addressing the junior Mrs. Rai, Neeru.

'But, *maa ji* . . .' began Neeru, when Radhika interrupted her.

'Mom, will it be ok if I escort Daadi Maa?' asked Radhika.

'But don't you want to go to Rajouri with me and Karan and visit your dad?' asked Neeru, looking surprised.

'Oh, you and dad will be busy attending parties every day, and all my friends have already left for various colleges in different cities,' said Radhika.

'Then that is settled, *bahu*. Radhika will go with me. And Bhanu and her grandson will also be there,' said Daadi Maa triumphantly.

'I know, Daadi Maa. Sunny told me about that and was most downcast, thinking he would be bored stiff,' said Radhika, suddenly realising that things were falling into place rather neatly for her. So, it was decided. Four seats were booked in the chair car of the *Vande Bharat Express*. Two were for Sunny and his grandmother and two were for Radhika and her grandmother. In the next few days,

Radhika found herself going around humming to herself. Her depression had lifted and her spirits had risen. She had begun to think that maybe if she visited the site of the places she had visited during her time travel, she might find some evidence to corroborate her fantastic story.

Chapter 27

It was on the first day of the Dusshera holidays. The Nizamuddin Railway Station was a bustle of activity. The little party from Noida had made its way early and immediately the train had come onto the platform, they had found their seats in the chair car and settled inside it. The interior of the train was really luxurious and posh, more like that of an aeroplane than of a train, with automated doors. The seats were comfortable beyond words. In each compartment, there were rows of two seaters on one side and three seaters on the other side of an aisle. They had tickets for two sets of two seaters. The two old ladies occupied one set, while Sunny and Radhika sat right behind them. The excitement of the old ladies was worth watching. They chattered away nineteen to the dozen. At last, the railway engine gave a hoot as the train finally left the station for Jhansi. As it slid out of Delhi, Radhika could hardly believe it. They were finally on their way to Jhansi!

Preparation for the trip had been made with a lot of enthusiasm on the part of the two old ladies. They had been thrilled to be planning a holiday together.

Immediately the train started, Sunny's grandmother, Mrs. Bhandari, took out a huge tiffin carrier from a duffle bag that she had stowed in the storage place above their heads.

'But I thought we had booked all the meals?' commented Radhika, looking puzzled.

'Oh, these are just a few snacks, my dear. Youngsters like you are generally hungry,' said Mrs. Bhandari, breezily proceeding to open it to reveal various mouth-watering snacks. Not to be outdone by her friend, whenever they stopped at a station, Radhika's Daadi Maa bought something to eat. *Murukku*, *chana-jor-garam*, salted peanuts, banana fritters, tea, Coca-Cola, sandwiches, *pakore*, they had them all. The two youngsters looked askance at their grandmothers but then had to smile as they realised that for the first time in their lives, the two ladies were having a ball of a time and enjoying themselves thoroughly. So much so that by the time lunch time came around, they all were too full to eat anything from the packed lunch handed out to them and had to keep it for later.

They reached Jhansi in the evening and found Surendra, the son of Daadi Maa's cousin, waiting at the station to take them home. As the train did not go to Babina, Sunny and his grandmother too got off at Jhansi. A young captain had come to pick them up and take them to Babina. Radhika and her grandmother promised to meet Sunny and his grandmother once the raising day festivities were over at Babina and their own registration, etc., had been completed.

'Yes. We'll shift into a hotel till the time we can go back together,' said Mrs. Bhandari.

With things finally settled, the two parties bade a temporary farewell to each other and separated, the Rai's to go with Surendra to the *haveli* and the Bhandaris to go on to Babina accompanied by the caption in the vehicle the regiment had sent.

Home turned out to be the ancient *haveli* Daadi Maa had talked about. It had a ground floor and a first floor. Part of the *haveli* had fallen down. But a portion of it, with about ten rooms, built in an F-formation, all connected by an open veranda around a courtyard, was still habitable and was occupied by the family of Daadi Maa's cousin. This portion had two courtyards. In one of them stood a huge, shady tree.

'That is a *badam* tree,' pointed out Surendra proudly.

'*Badam* tree? Here? I thought almonds grew in the hills,' commented Radhika. 'How nice to have your own almonds.'

Surendra looked embarrassed. 'Actually, you get huge kernels but there are no nuts inside,' he confessed.

'That is because, probably, this soil is not right for it. A *badam* tree requires hilly soil,' said the Daadi Maa. Everyone nodded.

There was a handpump under the tree, which provided the household with water. The bathroom was in one corner of the courtyard. The kitchen was in the corner opposite to the bathroom. The open veranda running along the courtyard connected it to the rest of the house and to a staircase that led up to the first floor of the *haveli*, which had two bedrooms, an enclosed veranda, a small bathroom, and a huge terrace. Another staircase from this open terrace led to the roof on top, which was shaded by a huge *peepal* tree.

As it was still warm, the men slept on the roof in the open, while the ladies slept in the courtyard below. All of them were welcomed with open arms by Daadi Maa's sister-in-law and the family of her younger son, Surendra, who lived with the parents. Daadi Maa's cousin brother had gone out for some work. Surendra had a teenage daughter, whom he introduced as Niti, and a younger son, Alok. Radhika found herself sharing a room with Niti. Daadi Maa had been given a room to herself.

After they had washed their hands and feet at the handpump, they all were led to a small wooden table, around which some chairs and a bench had been arranged, in the open veranda. Niti's mother made fresh *chapattis* in the small kitchen off the veranda, and Niti served everyone *chapatti, daal,* and two dry vegetables. They were also served home-made mango pickle kept in a stone *martaban*. Though the meal was simple, it was delicious.

Before they retired to sleep, each one of them was presented with a glass of hot milk the like of which Radhika had never tasted.

'It is from our own cows. We have two of them. A man comes every day to milk them morning and evening,' said Daadi Maa's sister-in-law with pride.

'No wonder it is so tasty, *bhaiya*,' said Daadi Maa to her cousin brother, who had returned from wherever he had gone. He had turned out to be older than Daadi Maa by quite a few years. Tall and thin, he looked tired and worn out. He was planning to go to his elder son, who resided in Canada, because Surendra wanted to shift with his family to a small flat in the town. He had gone out before to finalise some of the court work that would be done in the next few days.

By now, Radhika was feeling totally tired out and her eyes were nearly closed. String cots with mosquito nets had been arranged in the courtyard below for the ladies, and similar ones had been arranged for the men on the roof, above the first floor. Daadi Maa's cousin brother, whom they addressed as Daada ji, laughed when he saw Radhika eyeing the cots longingly and instructed his grandchildren to provide any help needed as everyone retired for the night. No one objected, and they fell asleep immediately their heads touched the pillows on the cots allotted to them.

Chapter 28

The next few days at the *haveli* were interesting for Radhika. The water for all their use was supplied by the handpump that stood in one corner of the outer courtyard and it needed to be worked hard. At first, Radhika thought it was fun, but soon, she had tired of it and also found her arms aching. The two toilets were attached to a septic tank and were very much like the one she had seen inside the fort back in 1857, during her time travel. Only now, they were made of white porcelain. Food was cooked mainly on a coal *angithi*, more out of habit than necessity because up until a few years back, gas was not easily available. That morning, Radhika's cousin uncle from Australia turned up and the two children of the fourth bother, that is, the youngest brother, also turned up and the house became really crowded.

Breakfast consisted of *poori*, vegetables, mango pickle, and extremely sweet, milky tea. Immediately it was over, preparations began for lunch. Daadi Maa and her cousins retired to the *baithak* to discuss how to go about getting to register the *haveli* on all their names. The net result was that a trip to the courts was made by Daadi Maa's cousins, Daadi Maa, Radhika, her cousin uncle and the two children of the fourth brother.

Radhika had never seen a court in her life except in movies. She did not know what she was expecting, but she was certainly not expecting what she saw there. There was no grand building and no grand chambers for the lawyers. Most of them sat under makeshift shelters made out of either plastic or aluminium. The shelters were without any walls, and all they contained were a few typewriters, some ancient cupboards, and a bench or two.

The lawyer they all had chosen seemed a little better off than the others. At least, he had a tiny room to himself. In this was crammed a desk with an old computer. Two benches occupied the rest of the room. While they all sat on the benches, the lawyer, obviously a *paan* eater, sat on a revolving chair on the other side of the desk. Behind him, on the wall, was a cheap calendar with the photo of Lord Ganesha. In one corner of the tiny room upon the wall was a tiny *mandir* with the idol of Goddess Laxmi in it. An obnoxiously scented *agarbatti* was stuck in a small brass container.

The lawyer made them all fill in a form typed on a 10-rupee stamp paper and attach copies of their duly self-attested Aadhar cards. Then he called in two men from outside and made them sign upon the forms as witnesses and paid them some money each. He sent the duly attested papers to the judge through his clerk, and then all they had to do was wait. It was boring, but they had no option. The room was stifling as the AC unit, although prominently on display upon the wall, was not working and there was only one fan, which was attached to one wall and so only the people sitting opposite it got any breeze. Although, thankfully, the weather was not too warm as it was already October, inside the small room, it was claustrophobic and hot. The lawyer was not helping matters much as he kept chewing *paan* throughout and every few minutes spat a stream of disgusting red liquid into an old rusted tin. Radhika was beginning to feel sick and thinking of walking out for some fresh air when the clerk returned and told them that the judge was ready to see them.

To Radhika's surprise, they never entered the chamber of the judge. They stood in a corridor outside while the judge sat inside a big air-conditioned room and looked at them through a small window. The corridor once again was very warm as none of the fans in it were working. Radhika found sweat literally pouring down her face as all the contenders for the *haveli* were made to go through a biometric identification to confirm that they were who they said they were. Then the judge ponderously read out the details filled in each form. He was so slow that Radhika could have screamed at him in frustration. As each person nodded in agreement with the details, he made them sign on the form once again and then the form was duly filed and a copy handed over to the person concerned. Thankfully, after that, they could all leave and go back to the *haveli*. Now, all they had to do was wait for a week–ten days for the registration to come through finally.

Chapter 29

Life in the *haveli* was slow and revolved around meals. To Radhika, it seemed as if all they did was cook, eat, drink, discuss food, and then repeat the cycle all day. The day began with bed tea, provided by Niti. Daadi Maa insisted on helping out in preparing breakfast, which usually consisted of *paranthe* and a spicy potato *bhaji*, as there were so many of them. After this, everyone dispersed for bathing and dressing up for the day as the maid who came part time washed up. Lunch consisted of *daal*, rice, and a dry vegetable, served with *papad*, *raita*, and pickles. Tea was served at five in the evening, when it was served with biscuits and some savoury snack. Dinner was served early, by eight, and consisted of one curry, one dry vegetable, and *chapattis*, rounded off with some sweet dish.

By now, even though she got along well enough with Niti, Radhika was thoroughly bored and eager to go and explore the old fort and palace that had belonged to the Rani of Jhansi, Laxmi Bai, with Sunny. She was eager to see if the place corresponded with what she had seen during her time travel. Sunny and his grandmother had shifted into their hotel, and Sunny was equally eager. He and Radhika talked every day on the cell phone. Radhika broached the subject at breakfast.

'I'll go by a taxi to the hotel where Sunny and his Daadi Maa are staying. From there, the two of us can go and see the Jhansi Fort and palace,' said Radhika.

'If you are going there, you can drop me off at the hotel. I would like to spend a day with my friend Bhanu,' said Daadi Maa immediately. Surendra, who worked as a deputy manager in a nationalised bank, offered to drop them at the hotel on his way to his bank.

'You can take a taxi from there to the fort in the city. They have a library and a museum inside the fort. After exploring the ruined palace, you can take a taxi back,' he said.

'Thank you, *bhaiya*!' exclaimed Radhika breaking into a smile.

The result was that the three of them went off in the old Maruti 800 that belonged to Surendra. Radhika had already talked to Sunny, so he was ready. His grandmother was delighted to see her friend. The two oldies were looking forward to spending the day together. After settling the two older ladies, Sunny and Radhika called for a taxi to take them to the fort in the city. They planned to explore the palace and the fort all day, have lunch somewhere there, have a look at the museum and return in a taxi in the evening.

Radhika was dying to show Sunny all the places she had visited during her time travel. The taxi turned out to be rather a dilapidated old Fiat, and the driver was a cheerful, garrulous fellow by the name of Shah Nawaz Khan. He kept up a running commentary upon all the places they were passing by. Apparently, he was used to taking tourists around Jhansi and was well versed in the history of the city. He cheerfully informed them that his ancestors had been Pathans who had fought alongside the rani during the Great War of 1857, which he said had been given the name of a mutiny or a rebellion by the British to downgrade its importance.

The fort was located upon a small hillock. As they approached it through the narrow streets of the old town, Radhika could feel excitement mounting inside her. She could vividly remember how the rani and all her lady friends had many a times ridden along these lanes and had even fought in them on the final day while fleeing from the fort. For a few moments, she was back in 1857, with all the dust, deafening sounds of explosions, and the awful smell of gunpowder hanging in the air. Sunny snapped his fingers in front of her eyes and laughingly said, 'Will you stop dreaming. Where are you?'

'Err . . . I am not dreaming!' protested Radhika. 'I was just looking forward to seeing the famous fortress of Jhansi ki Rani.'

The taxi driver smiled at the excitement in her voice. 'I am afraid you might find it rather disappointing. The ASI has taken over a part of it and are trying to restore it. Except for the library and the little museum there, there is hardly anything else to see.'

'We'll see,' commented Radhika.

Finally, they stopped at one of the gates of the fort. It had been known earlier and even now was known as the Orchha Gate. The taxi driver offered to wait for them there so that when they had finished sightseeing, he could take them back. They first refused but, then when he insisted, Sunny told him to return for them at four o'clock. 'We should have finished by then,' he said and turning they entered the fort. As Radhika and Sunny started walking up a winding road, Radhika remembered how grand the gate used to be when she had been last there. This was the gate Rao Dulhaju had opened when he had betrayed the rani and let the British soldiers inside the fort, because of which the rani had had to flee from Jhansi in the dead of the night. Radhika remembered fighting alongside Munder at the gate, how Munder had jumped down after Rao Dulhaju and killed him with one stroke of her sword but had been unable to shut the gate once again as it had been too heavy. She had died yelling to Radhika to rush and inform the rani about the betrayal.

For a few moments, Radhika was back in that time, that night, the deafening sounds, the screams, the shouts, how she had jumped upon her horse tethered to a tree a little way back and how she had raced to warn the rani. To her, it seemed as if it was just yesterday.

'Hey, where are you?' asked Sunny, snapping his finger in front of Radhika's eyes again, as she had halted and seemed frozen where she stood. Radhika came back to the present with a shudder and shook herself.

'I was just remembering the last time I was here. The noise, the dust, the . . . it seems to me like a dream,' shuddered Radhika.

'Snap out of it, Rats,' said Sunny. 'That's what we are here for. To prove that you did not dream it all but all that actually took place,' he said.

Radhika immediately glared at him. 'Don't you call me Rats. You know how I hate that name,' she said, sounding mad.

Sunny laughed. He had achieved his aim of bringing her back to the present.

'Ok, ok,' he laughed, putting up his hands in mock defence. Radhika realised what he had been up to and gave a reluctant smile back. Then, they entered the gate.

As the two of them walked towards the palace, Radhika described to Sunny all that had passed on that fatal night, how Munder had killed Rao Dulhaju and been killed herself fighting bravely till her last breath and Radhika's own mad dash for the palace to warn the queen that the walls had been breached, that she had been betrayed by a traitor.

'Weren't you scared?' asked Sunny, looking at her in amazement.

'Where was the time to be scared? Too much was happening,' said Radhika simply.

Sunny gave her shoulders a squeeze, and they started walking once again.

They passed a small temple on the way. It was the famous Gauri Temple, where the rani had always come to pray. It had been so grand and beautiful then. It was where the rani had met her look alike, Jhalkari, for the first time, during the festival of Haldi Kumkum, as Radhika had been told by her ancestor Ganga. Ganga had described it in detail: how the rani had celebrated the ceremony of Haldi Kumkum at this *mandir*. At that time, it had been so vibrant and alive. Now, the temple looked shabby and neglected.

Radhika and Sunny reached the palace. It also had a look of neglect. There was a small room, with an office occupied by a curator, who asked them whether they wanted an audio guide or not. They refused. Radhika was sure she would be able to go around on her own. As she and Sunny wandered around, Radhika felt a real sense of déjà vu. She could hardly believe that she had been walking through these very chambers just a few weeks back. At that time, they had vibrated with life. So many people had lived in the palace, and there was forever some activity or the other going on. How different it had been then! Now, the chambers looked so neglected and dilapidated. The two of them came to the audience chamber, where she remembered having first met Tatya Tope and the other *sardars* – the same chamber where the rani had given audience to the British residents.

Radhika stood rooted to the spot in front of the throne. The almost-transparent curtains it had been hidden behind in that time were no longer there. The rani had sat behind the curtains and she, Radhika, had stood behind her, along with her other *sahelis*. She could almost hear the echo of the rani's strong voice as she declared vehemently, '*Main apni Jhansi kabhi nahin doongi!*' (I will never give up my Jhansi!).

When they reached what had constituted the private wing of the rani, where she had resided, to their dismay, they found a thick rope cordoning it off. A badly-written sign stated that no one was allowed beyond this as restoration work was going on by the ASI. This was a blow.

'Oh no! How do I show you where the yuvraj's room was?' exclaimed Radhika.

'Looks like we won't be able to confirm anything,' said Sunny, looking disappointed.

'Let us just lift the rope and go ahead,' suggested Radhika.

'Don't be such an idiot! If someone catches us, we'll be in real hot water,' said Sunny.

'Stop being such a scaredy-cat!' said Radhika. She had just lifted the thick rope and slipped under it when they heard someone whistling. Both of them froze. Even as they stood there, a boy in his twenties came around a bend in the passage. Dressed in jeans and a blue t-shirt, he had a checkered cap upon his head. He had sharp, delicate features. He was the one who had been whistling. He halted upon catching sight of them.

'Hello! This portion of the palace is out of bounds. Haven't they put a notice to that effect?' he exclaimed in a little high-pitched voice.

'Yes, they have,' said Radhika, looking guilty.

'Then what are you doing this side of the rope?' demanded the boy, looking belligerently at them.

'We just wanted to see this part of the palace,' blurted out Radhika.

'Well, you can't. It is under renovation,' said the boy.

Till now, Sunny had been looking suspiciously at the boy. Suddenly, he burst out, 'Hey! You are not a boy! You are a girl!'

The person looked scornfully at him. 'Of course, I am. Dr. Shalini Mehta at your service.' And taking off her cap, she bowed theatrically and laughed good humouredly.

Suddenly, things clicked. Of course, she was the visiting faculty who had given that lecture and taken that seminar on the Battle of 1857 at Delhi University, which she and Sunny had attended.

Radhika stared at the girl bewildered. But she looked so different! That Dr. Mehta had been distinctly middle aged, dressed in a cotton *saree* and with a loose bun at the nape of her neck. This Dr. Mehta looked more like the girl she remembered. She sported a mop of short, boyish hair. She was fairly tall and, with a boyish figure and dressed in scruffy jeans and a T-shirt, she looked ten years younger and more like an urchin than a professor of archaeology.

'Are you the Dr. Mehta who came to Delhi University some six months back to take a seminar on the First War of Independence in 1857?' asked Radhika cautiously, just to confirm. She was having some doubts.

Dr. Mehta looked a little astonished. 'I am the very same person. Do you know me?'

'We attended your lecture, *didi*,' said Radhika excitedly. 'But you looked so different.'

Shalini Mehta raised an eyebrow. '*Didi*?'

Radhika looked abashed. 'You are the daughter of General P. K. Mehta of artillery.'

'How do you know me?' asked Shalini Mehta, looking in surprise at Radhika.

'Actually, I don't think you remember me but your father was my father's first CO and then later his brigade commander. You were all of twenty-five and I was five, and usually you were left in charge of all the kids when there was an official party,' blurted out Radhika.

'You are . . . ?' Shalini looked enquiringly at her.

'I am Radhika Rai, daughter of Brigadier Rai,' said Radhika.

Shalini's face cleared up and she gave a grin. 'Now I remember. You were all such brats and me being the eldest army brat had to look after all of you whenever there was a party on. And you all were such a pain . . .'

'No, we weren't, *didi*. We loved you because we had so much fun with you,' countered Radhika, smiling.

Shalini stepped forward and suddenly gave her an unexpected hug. Radhika hugged her back happily.

'*Didi*, that day in DU, you looked so different. I hardly recognised you,' said Radhika.

'I have cut my hair since then and I only wear a *saree* when I have to attend seminars or go to a formal party,' said Shalini Mehta, smiling mischievously.

'Now, come along. I'll treat you both to a cup of our canteen's best *chai* and some hot *samosas*. I want to know all about your parents. And you had a baby brother. He must be big by now,' said Shalini, smiling at the two of them and shaking their hands and then leading them outside, towards the back of the library, where there was a small canteen.

Chapter 30

Very soon, the three of them were sitting together in the little canteen and talking nineteen to the dozen over hot *samosas* and extremely sweet tea.

Shalini Mehta asked after Brigadier Rai and his wife and told Radhika that she worked for the Archaeological Survey of India and was in charge of the renovation project going on in the palace. Radhika found herself pouring out her bizarre adventure story, which Shalini heard out in silence.

As she told the young archaeologist all about her experience in time travel. Shalini's eyes opened wide, and the look of astonishment on her face was very evident. But to Radhika's and Sunny's surprise, she did not pooh-pooh the entire episode as just a bit of hallucination.

'I say! What luck! I wish I had been with you. I could have got first-hand knowledge of that time in history,' she said wistfully.

They all smiled at this. 'But what am I to do now? If we cannot find that passage into the room that belonged to the yuvraj, how do I prove to the world that I really travelled in time? That dastardly Dr. Dastoor has stolen all my *mohars* and declared that he found them in his own grandmother's collection of coins! And to top it, he has gone off on leave and is not even here,' almost wailed Radhika.

'You are wrong, Radhika. He is very much here. In fact, he is one of the visiting faculties who keep dropping at the site of the excavation and renovation from time to time. Many days, he and another of his *changus* sit in the library and go through old manuscripts. I only wish they would stay there, but he has the bad habit of wandering all over where he has no business to be wandering about. Unfortunately, my boss is a friend of his. But as far as I know, Dr. Dastoor has not come in today. He is not a very pleasant person. He throws his weight around and thinks that just because I am a woman, I am incompetent and a fool,' almost spat out Shalini.

'Oh no!' exclaimed both Radhika and Sunny together, looking dismayed. 'What do we do now?'

'I suggest we first try and find that passage that goes from the *pilkhana* to the yuvraj's room,' said Shalini slowly.

'But how? You all have cordoned that area off,' complained Radhika.

'You will come with me, stupid. Only, we must try not to let anyone see us or they may ask questions and may complain against me to my seniors for taking unauthorised people inside the cordoned-off area. Especially, if Dr. Dastoor was to see, he would love to make trouble for me,' said Shalini with a smile.

Very soon, they were back in the palace and having made sure that no one was around, had reached the cordoned-off area. They quickly ducked under the rope barrier and then walked quickly down the corridor with bated breaths until they had turned a corner and were out of sight of the other part of the palace. Still stepping stealthily, lest any other colleague of Shalini should suddenly come upon them and question their presence there, they finally reached the room that Radhika distinctly remembered had been occupied by Damodar Rao, the yuvraj.

Radhika was sad to see how dilapidated the room looked now. The furnishings were either broken or tarnished and the curtains, etc., were almost in tatters. Surprisingly, the tapestry behind which the entrance to the passage was located was still there, although it had faded a lot.

Excited beyond words, Radhika raced up to it and lifted it up triumphantly and then stood rooted to the spot, in shock. There was no opening in the wall. There was just the wall itself.

'What's the matter?' asked Shalini, coming up behind her.

'It is not there,' said Radhika almost in a whisper.

'What is not there?' asked Sunny, also coming up.

'The entrance to the secret passage,' said Radhika in a hollow voice.

Meanwhile, Shalini was examining the wall behind the tapestry and now she traced an outline with her forefinger.

'It has been bricked up, my dear. See, this part of the wall is newer than the rest of it.'

Radhika let out a sigh of relief. For a moment there, she had felt as though it had all indeed been a dream. 'What do we do now?' she asked turning to her new-found friend.

'I'll try and tell my boss to get this part broken open,' said Shalini.

'But, I say, in the meanwhile, what about trying to dig up the box you buried in the garden with the yuvraj?' said Sunny suddenly.

'Does it have anything special to show that it comes from the time of the rani?' asked Shalini with interest.

'There is a letter in English from the rani in it, along with a quill embossed with the name of the rani, which she used to write with, and some toys,' said Radhika, sounding excited once again.

'Can we go and dig it up?' asked Sunny. Shalini was a little hesitant. 'I suggest we dig once the area has been closed to the public for the day. Otherwise, a lot of questions may be asked,' said Shalini.

'But how can we get in after closing hours?' asked Radhika in dismay. 'That's a point,' said Sunny.

'They have a sound-and-light show every evening. I suggest you both come, attend it, and while it is going on, slip away,' suggested Shalini.

'But can we bring in some instruments to dig?' asked Sunny anxiously.

'Leave that to me. We'll go along just now and find some and hide them near the place, ready to be recovered in the evening. But do get torches with you,' said Shalini.

Chapter 31

Having decided on the course of action, the three of them walked towards where Radhika remembered the small garden to be. It was right next to the library-cum-museum. As they entered the park, Radhika excitedly pointed out the corner where the peepal tree, now huge, stood. Under it, there was a stone bench.

'I am sure that's the place where we buried the *paan-daan*. At that time, that peepal tree had been small. Obviously, it has grown over time,' she commented, starting towards it. Shalini caught hold of her arm.

'Hold on. You can't just go and start digging there in broad daylight. That spot is clearly visible from the library. Anyone can see us. Remember what we decided.'

'It is so frustrating!' exclaimed Radhika in despair.

'Come on. It is safer to wait till when the complex is closed and most people have gone home. Even if Dr. Dastoor is not staying on the premises – he is staying in a hotel in the town I think – someone might see us and just tell him,' said Shalini.

'I suggest you both go on to the library and the museum just now and meet me at around seven in the evening outside the library. Generally, there are no guards on duty around this place at that time,' said Shalini. 'By the way, the Hindi version of the sound-and-light show is very good. I suggest you come over to see that as people are more engrossed in it and there is a bigger crowd for it and you will find it easier to slip away without being noticed.'

So, the three of them split up, having fixed to meet up later in the evening.

'We'll have to tell them at home that we are coming to see the sound-and-light show here,' said Radhika, as they made their way towards the library-cum-museum.

'We'll ask our friendly taxi driver to pick us up,' said Sunny.

Inside the library, they were asked to sign a register. They had to state the reason for their visit as a temporary pass had to be made for them. Radhika had lifted the pen to sign her name when she suddenly froze.

'What's the matter?' asked Sunny. 'Why are you looking at the register as if you have seen a ghost?'

Radhika only pointed towards a name just a few names above where they were signing. Sunny looked and then he also looked grim. Dr. Dastoor had signed in just an hour before them, and he had not yet signed out.

'I don't want to meet him,' said Radhika, almost in a panic.

'Then let us go to the museum first,' suggested Sunny.

The two of them walked out of the library and towards the back of it, where the museum was located. The museum turned out to be rather drab and not too well kept. There were just two rooms, and most of the artefacts were inside glass cases that needed dusting. They had gone through the artefacts in barely half an hour. They were now at a loss what to do. With nothing else to do, they decided to go to the library, deciding to take a chance that Dr. Dastoor would not see them even if he was there. Radhika went towards the desk to sign her name while Sunny went off to the washroom.

Radhika was signing her name when someone approached her from behind. Then, to her utter horror, she heard the raspy voice of Dr. Dastoor as he addressed her.

'Hello. Fancy meeting you here. What are you doing here?' he asked.

Radhika froze. Then she turned around slowly and there stood the hateful man smirking at her.

Radhika's mind went blank. She wanted to lash out at the man and demand how he had had the gumption to steal the *mohars* she had given him for authentication, but her body seemed to have frozen. The man did not look even a little abashed.

'What are you doing here?' asked Dr. Dastoor once again. He sounded most banal.

'How dare you? hissed Radhika at him through clenched teeth. 'You stole the *mohars* I gave you to authenticate, you scoundrel!'

Dr. Dastoor laughed. 'Oh that! No one would have believed your story, lady. Wasn't it better I lent it my name for credibility? You should thank me for it.'

Radhika could not believe the blatant declaration she was hearing. The cheek of the man! He was justifying his robbery. It was too much. 'Get out of my way before I start screaming!' threatened Radhika. Just then, Sunny came out of the washroom and seeing Radhika in what seemed like a heated argument with someone, halted. He bunched up his fists, sensing that something was wrong.

The moment Dr. Dastoor saw a third person entering the scene, he just turned and walked out of the library. Radhika let out her breath and sagged against the counter. She had not been aware that she had been holding onto her breath. By now, the man in charge of the counter had sensed that something was wrong and had come out from behind it.

'Is everything all right, lady?' he asked, looking in concern at the pale face of Radhika. 'Was that gentleman troubling you in any way?'

Radhika gave him a tumultuous smile. 'It is ok.'

By now Sunny, had also come up and was looking in concern at her.

'Are you alright?' he also asked. 'And who was that? He looked kind of familiar.'

'Dr. Dastoor,' was all that Radhika could whisper.

'Don't tell me he had the audacity to confront you!' said Sunny, looking in disbelief at the fast-disappearing figure of the man.

'I'll just go and . . .' and he would have dashed off after Dr. Dastoor but Radhika caught hold of his hand.

'Don't. The man is bad. I don't want him to know that I have any kind of support. As it is, he is sure to know I am onto something. He doesn't know I am with someone. I am only glad that when I was telling him my story, I forgot to tell him all about the incident with the yuvraj,' said she.

Once inside the library, Radhika looked around for old books and suddenly spotted a book that she was sure she had seen earlier. She quietly picked it up, and a piece of paper fell out of it. It was the map the yuvraj had made that day when they both had buried the box. She was jubilant. She showed it to Sunny and then finally, the two of them decided to just go back home and come back again, in the evening, for the sound-and-light show.

Chapter 32

In the evening, the taxi driver Shah Nawaz Khan picked up Radhika, Sunny, and the two old grandmothers along with them to take them for the sound-and-light show. To their dismay, the two older ladies had insisted on accompanying the youngsters.

'We'll have to be careful how we slip out from the show. I don't really know what our grandmothers will think of all this about digging up in the garden, etc.,' whispered Radhika to Sunny when she had an opportunity.

At the palace, they found a good crowd of tourists gathered to see the show. Shah Nawaz Khan told them that he would wait for them in the car park and left them at the entrance. 'You give me a ring when it is over, and I will pick you up from here,' he said, giving his cell phone number to Sunny.

Sunny bought the tickets, and they all walked into the palace. They walked through many corridors and courtyards. Some of them Radhika recognised from her sojourn before. Finally, they came to one that was open but surrounded on three sides by rooms. Radhika remembered that this was where the rani had taught the girls sword fighting, wrestling, and *malkhamb*. For a few moments, Radhika was gripped by a wave of nostalgia. After all, she had also practiced here with the others for quite some time and had taught them self-defence. Now, there were chairs arranged for the people to sit upon and obviously the sound-and-light show was going to be woven around the area. Washrooms for the visitors had been erected towards the back.

Radhika and Sunny had already decided that once the show began, they would slip away on the pretext of going to the washroom and they would be back before the show ended. Shalini had promised to wait for them near the entrance of the library.

All the seats were full, and there was a lot of chitchat and excitement in the air. Everyone was looking forward to the show, which had been touted as one of the best of its kind. Both the old ladies were equally excited and chattered away nineteen to the dozen. At last, as the sun finally set and darkness fell, the lights dimmed and there was a roll of drums. The show had begun.

Ten minutes into the show, Radhika whispered to her Daadi Maa that she was going to visit the washroom and got up and edged her way out of the line of seats. Seeing her, Sunny also followed. The two older ladies frowned. 'Really, children these days get bored so easily,' thought Mrs. Rai senior.

Radhika swiftly went towards the back of the courtyard and then slipped away. Sunny followed her and caught up with her. They reached the library and looked around apprehensively. They could hear the music and sound of the sound-and-light show in the far distance, but all was quiet here.

A small shadow detached itself from some dark shadows on the side and approached them. A light flared as Shalini switched on an emergency lantern operated by a battery. She had also brought along a spade to dig with.

'Where did you get that?' asked Sunny in surprise.

'Some workers must have left it around,' replied Shalini, unlatching the gate to the little park next to the library. 'I just picked it up.'

'Come on,' said Radhika. 'Let us not waste time. We have to return to our seats before the show gets over.'

The other two followed her. Once inside the park, Shalini closed the gate once again and they quickly went over to the tree that Radhika had pointed out in the day time. Shalini set the lamp on one side and picked up the spade.

'We'll take turns,' said Radhika.

'Certainly not!' said Sunny, taking the spade from her. 'I'll do the honours.'

The spade was heavy and the ground hard. It took Sunny all his strength to dig. After some time, Radhika insisted on relieving him and he thankfully handed the spade to her.

'How much do we have to dig?' asked Sunny, wiping sweat from his brow.

'Well . . . , the yuvraj insisted on burying the box quite deep and I suppose the layers of mud have only increased over the years,' panted Radhika as she dug. Suddenly, there was a clang as the spade hit something metallic.

'We have found it,' gasped Radhika with supressed excitement. Sunny was bending over the hole they had dug while Shalini had picked up the lamp and was shining it down into the hole. There it was! The brass *paan-daan*. Of course, it had turned totally black with grime, but it still looked solidly intact. Sunny put his hands down into the hole and struggled to pull it up. It suddenly came up with a rush, and he fell back with a thump.

Radhika and Shalini crowded around Sunny and almost snatched the brass box from him. Radhika opened it with shaking hands. As the lid fell open, she saw that things inside were as intact as she had put them in more than a hundred and fifty years earlier. She picked up the silk upon which the rani had written and gently placed it on the side, not sure if it would crack and disintegrate after having been stored for so many years. The wooden toys belonging to the yuvraj smiled up at her from the bottom of the box. There was the quill belonging to the queen also. Radhika suddenly found her throat blocked with tears. She wondered what had happened to the little boy, to whom she had told so many stories and who had been so sweet. She had heard that he had survived the freedom struggle of 1857 and gone on to fight the British for a pension of rupees five, which had not been granted to him till his death, sometime in 1906.

Shalini sat on the ground and reverently, with extreme care, unrolled the rani's letter. The writing, though faded over the years, was still legible. Shalini read it, and the look of wonder upon her face deepened. All the while she was reading, she was muttering. 'Oh my God! What a find! What a find!'

'This is proof that the rani knew English,' said Radhika in triumph.

'Yes, my dear. I'll produce it in front of my faculty,' declared Shalini and was beginning to roll it up again when there was a sound. At first, it did not register with the trio sitting on the ground, so occupied were they with their find. Then, a hand snatched the missive from Shalini's hands and a menacing voice broke the silence, 'No, you won't be producing this in front of the world as your find. I will be.'

The three on the ground froze. They were stunned. 'Don't move, any of you. I have you covered with my gun. Hand over the box, along with its contents,' continued the voice menacingly.

Slowly the three on the ground turned as one, but all they could see in the light of the emergency lamp was two tall dark shadows. Both of them wore masks, like the ones popular during the COVID-19 pandemic.

The taller of the two men was holding a gun, while the shorter one came and quickly snatched the box from Shalini's hands.

'No!' almost shouted Shalini, as she desperately tried to hold onto it, but the taller man grabbed her hair and pulling her against himself, hit her hand with his gun. Shalini gave a scream and let go of the box. In the struggle, the taller man's mask slid down and all of them looked in shock at him.

'You!' exclaimed Radhika, turning and glaring at him.

'Dr. Dastoor! What are you doing here?' cried out Shalini, struggling to turn and look at his face above hers.

Sunny made a move as if he would fling himself upon the two men, but Dr. Dastoor backed away hastily, holding on to Shalini and dragging her. He pressed his gun to her temple and said between grated teeth, 'Don't even move, young man, or I will be forced to shoot this young lady,' he threatened menacingly. 'Bholu, tie their hands. Then, let us put them where they will not be found for a long, long time,' he ordered his companion and smiled evilly at them.

'But you will not escape, Dr. Dastoor. When we get free, we will denounce you and tell the world how you have been stealing the discoveries of other people and passing them off as your own for years,' said Radhika scornfully.

Dr. Dastoor laughed maliciously. 'That is, if you ever get free. Maybe I will put you in a place from where you never get out and about which no one knows. You three will just have vanished off the face of earth, without any trace, my dear, and I will be hailed as the discoverer of some magnificent facts about the Rani of Jhansi. What a sensation I will cause.'

By then, the second man, whom Dr. Dastoor had addressed as Bholu, produced a ball of raw string from his pocket and proceeded to tie up each one's hands behind their back. He took pleasure in tying up their hands so tightly that the string cut into their flesh, making them wince with pain. He also took out a dirty *gamchha* and tearing it into three pieces gagged the three helpless friends with the pieces. Radhika almost gagged upon the stench coming from the *gamchha*. Obviously, the man had not washed it in ages.

'Now, get them up and follow me while I lead with this lady to the place where no one will ever find them. Someone may find them eventually, but that would be many years later, and they would only find their skeletons,' said Dr. Dastoor with relish. Very soon, the three prisoners were stumbling along with their captors. The man addressed as Bholu had picked up the emergency light and taken it along. Radhika realised that they were going away from the palace.

Radhika wondered where they were being taken. They stumbled through narrow lanes that were deserted and then Radhika realised that they were making for the *pilkhana*. They reached it with only one mishap, when someone came down the street and Dr. Dastoor shoved them into a doorway until the person had passed by.

'Don't try and attract any attention, otherwise I'll be forced to shoot not only you all but also the person passing by,' threatened Dr. Dastoor in a whisper.

They reached the old *pilkhana*, which was actually a tourist site. There was a rope barrier, which Dr. Dastoor lifted up and pushed the three of them inside. He pushed them to the back of the *pilkhana* and around a big rock set in the wall of the *pilkhana* and Radhika knew immediately where he was going to imprison them – inside the hidden passage, the passage that led to what had been the room of the yuvraj. But now, that entrance to the yuvraj's room had been sealed.

Dr. Dastoor herded them all towards the entrance of the passage, which now boasted a heavy door with solid padlocks, obviously recently installed to deter any adventurous soul from wandering into the tunnel, and then smiled evilly. 'I am going to lock you all inside here and throw away the key where no one will find it. By the way, shouting will not help you all since no one visits the *pilkhana* anymore. It is out of bounds for everyone.'

The three prisoners looked at him in horror. Sunny started struggling and so did the other two, but it was of no use. Dr. Dastoor just shoved them inside the ancient passage so hard that they all fell on the hard floor. Radhika hit her head on the opposite wall and nearly choked on her gag.

'Before we go, frisk them for any kind of sharp instruments and cell phones. I don't want them contacting anyone if they manage to free themselves,' ordered Dr. Dastoor.

His sidekick frisked them all and took all their cell phones. Then, Dr. Dastoor turned to leave and said jovially, 'I'll be kind to you and leave this lamp for you all. Enjoy till the battery lasts,' and setting the lamp down beside them, Dr. Dastoor gave a theatrical salute and he and his helper stepped out of the passage and shut the heavy door. The prisoners heard a grating sound and realised that the door had been bolted from outside. Then they heard the distinct sounds of the lock being put.

Chapter 33

The three prisoners looked at each other in the feeble light of the emergency light. Radhika was bleeding from where her forehead had split open when she had hit it on the rough stonewall. For some time, the three of them sat in utter despair, not knowing what to do. Then, Shalini rolled herself over to where Radhika sat with her back to the wall. She motioned to Radhika that Radhika should lie down on the floor and then, turning her back towards her, struggled to pull off the gag tied on Radhika's mouth. She managed it after some struggle. Thankfully, Radhika spat out the dirty cloth and then did the same for Shalini. Then, the two girls did the same for Sunny. At least they could talk now.

'Thank God for small mercies,' said Radhika fervently.

'We must try and get out from here,' said Sunny.

'Yes. But how?' asked Shalini in disgust.

'You must have guessed that this is the secret passage that leads from the *pilkhana* to the room that the yuvraj used to occupy,' said Radhika.

'But that entrance has been bricked up,' said Shalini in despair.

'First and foremost, we have to free ourselves. Then we may be able to force the door that that crook has locked,' said Sunny.

'Let me try and open your bonds,' offered Shalini to Radhika. The other two nodded. The two girls sat back to back, and Shalini began trying to open the string, but the knots were too tight. Soon, her fingers had started to bleed. At last, she fell back in despair. All of them looked beaten.

'When we get out of here, I'll see to it that that fraud goes behind bars,' growled Shalini.

'That is if we ever manage to get out,' said Radhika in despair.

'Our grandmothers must be frantic, wondering where we have vanished to,' said Sunny suddenly.

'Oh my God! I had forgotten all about them,' said Radhika, almost in tears.

They sat there, wallowing in despair, when suddenly Shalini cocked her head to one side. She listened carefully and then whispered. 'I think there is someone outside the door.'

'Has that villain returned?' asked Radhika, looking scared.

'Why will he return? By now, he must be trying to get as far away from this place as possible,' said Sunny.

Just then, a soft voice whispered from outside. 'Is anyone inside? Radhika *beta* . . .'

'Daadi Maa!' almost yelled Radhika and forgetting that her hands were still tied tried to get up and fell over.

'Yes, both me and Bhanu are here, *beta*. But how do we open this door? There is a huge lock upon it, and there is no key,' replied Mrs. Rai senior from outside.

'How did you find us, Daadi Maa?' yelled out Radhika. The other two were equally excited. 'Well . . . we followed you when you went to the washroom as we also wanted to visit it and were astonished to see that you were going somewhere else. We saw everything that happened inside the park and followed you all here.'

'What exactly were you three up to?' asked Mrs. Rai.

Radhika decided that she would have to give some sort of quick explanation and so gave a short summary of her time travel and what had happened since, with both grandmothers listening quietly in astonishment.

'Can you get help? We are tied up inside here,' called out Sunny finally.

There was a hurried consultation outside. Then Sunny's grandmother, Mrs. Bhandari, called out, 'Help? From where?' sounding confused.

'Daadi Maa, get hold of Khan, our taxi driver,' called out Sunny. 'He'll definitely help you.'

'How do I contact him?' asked Mrs. Bhandari. 'I don't have his number.'

'Oh no! His number was in my mobile, which that brute took,' said Sunny.

'You will have to go to the taxi stand personally,' said Radhika.

'Please go fast. The battery lamp is not going to last long. Very soon, there will be no light even,' said Shalini, sounding nervous.

'Don't panic, children. We'll be back with help soon,' called out Radhika's grandmother and then there was silence outside.

The three prisoners sagged with relief. Help was on its way, and they could relax.

Ten minutes later, two very excited old ladies reached where all the taxies were parked. The taxies were parked in rows, and most of the drivers were sitting around in groups, drinking tea from a nearby *dhaba* or just gossiping. The two old friends wondered how they would ever find their taxi driver? Ultimately, they didn't have to actually do that themselves. Their driver, who was drinking a glass of hot tea, spotted them. He swallowed his tea in a hurry, nearly burning his mouth, and came over quickly to them.

'*Arey maa ji*, what are you doing here? Why didn't you give me a ring? I'd have come and picked you up,' exclaimed Shah Nawaz Khan. The two old ladies were really thankful to see him. Very soon, they were trying to tell him all that had happened. They were so excited that it came out in rather a garbled way. In the end, Khan made them sit on a string cot near the *dhaba* and brought hot tea for both of them and then asked them to tell their story once again. By now, a whole lot of drivers from other taxis had also gathered around and were listening in.

'You tell the story, as it is mainly your granddaughter's story,' said Mrs. Bhandari to the Mrs. Rai and sat back to sip her tea. So, Mrs. Rai told them about how her granddaughter had taken some *mohars* that had been in the family since the time of Rani Laxmi Bai for authentication to Dr. Dastoor and how he had fleeced her and passed them off as his own find. Actually, Radhika had warned her earlier on about not even breathing to anyone about her time travel, lest people label her mad and not believe her. Instead, she told them about the map Radhika had discovered inside the book in the library and how she, Sunny and their new friend had decided to dig for the treasure it had listed upon it.

As the agog taxi drivers listened to the story, Mrs. Rai told them how she and her friend had followed the two children, what had happened in the park, and how the villainous Dr. Dastoor, along with a sidekick and on the point of a gun, had taken all of them prisoner to some place in the old city and locked them up inside what seemed to be a room with an old stout door.

'We have to break the lock and rescue them,' ended Mrs. Rai.

'Can you take us to the police?' asked Mrs. Bhandari.

'The police will take too much time and ask too many questions,' declared one of the drivers.

'We cannot leave the three tied up inside that room till then,' said another.

'Fetch a crowbar,' ordered Shah Nawaz Khan, taking charge.

Within minutes, four burly taxi drivers armed with crowbars and sticks were accompanying the two ladies.

On the way, they kept a look out for Dr. Dastoor and his sidekick but obviously the villains had left the area with their loot and gone back to wherever they were staying.

Chapter 34

Inside the tunnel, the three prisoners were waiting impatiently to be rescued. Suddenly, the emergency light flickered and then went off.

'Oh no!' exclaimed Radhika, immediately beginning to feel scared.

'Don't feel scared. We are three of us here, and our grandmas should be here any time, along with help,' Sunny tried to bolster her courage.

'I wish they would hurry up. Unfortunately, the taxi stand is at the other side of the complex,' informed Shalini regretfully.

'I only hope they find it quickly. It might be difficult in the night,' said Radhika.

'Come on, let us play *antakshari*,' suggested Shalini in a bid to keep up their spirit. So, in the pitch dark, the three of them tried to play the game, but none of them was a good singer and they gave up the game after some time.

'That brute has tied my hands so tightly that the string is hurting and my hands are nearly numb,' groaned Radhika after some time.

'So are mine,' said Shalini.

'Let us decide what we are going to do once we are rescued,' suggested Sunny, trying to distract the two girls.

'We must catch that scoundrel and recover that box,' said Radhika promptly.

'We must complain to the police and ensure he is put behind bars,' said Shalini.

'If I get my hand upon that bastard, I am going to relish just bashing him up,' declared Sunny.

'But I have a feeling the crook will leave Jhansi as fast as he can,' said Shalini, sounding gloomy.

'Yes. He'll want to present his robbery as his find to the press in Delhi,' added Radhika.

'Do hurry up, grandma,' muttered Sunny, sounding frustrated beyond measure.

Just then, they heard the sound of many feet. Then, someone was at the door, banging away at the lock on the door. Within a minute, the lock was broken and the door thrown open and a torch was shown in.

'Thank God, Daadi Maa!' exclaimed both Radhika and Sunny simultaneously to their individual grandmothers as they saw four burly men standing at the opening of the passage with crowbars and sticks and the two beloved faces peeping from behind them. Two of the men entered the passage, and the ropes of the captives were thankfully cut.

The three captives rubbed their wrists together to get their circulation going, wincing with pain as feeling returned to their hands.

'There is no time to lose, children. We must stop that crook from getting away,' said Mrs. Rai.

'*Maa ji*, have you all any idea where that man is staying?' asked Shah Nawaz Khan suddenly.

'Why?' asked Mrs. Rai.

'He will definitely go there to collect his luggage before he leaves Jhansi. We can get hold of him there,' said the taxi driver.

'I know where he is staying. It is the guest house belonging to the Archaeological Survey of India,' said Shalini and gave the address.

'Come on then. Let us go,' said Shah Nawaz Khan to his friends.

'Wait. Shouldn't we call in the police?' asked Mrs. Bhandari.

'By the time the police arrive, it might be too late. The bird might have flown,' said Sunny.

'He will no doubt also claim that the box is his finding,' said one of the drivers.

'There is a train for Delhi at ten. I think he plans to catch that,' said one of the drivers.

'Daadi Maa, you both go to the police station and get help. We all will go with our friends here and see what we can do in the meanwhile,' declared Sunny.

At first, the taxi drivers were not too happy about separating, but then in the end gave in. The result was that fifteen minutes later, one fully loaded taxi left the fort for the Archaeological Survey of India's guest house while one with the two old ladies went towards the police station to register a complaint and bring help if possible.

The guest house belonging to the Archaeological Survey of India turned out to be an old, small, single-storied bungalow. At one time, it had been the mess for the British soldiers stationed in Jhansi. It was one of the few relics of the British era still in use. It stood in its own grounds, and it was obvious that they were rather neglected, as tall grass and shrubs were everywhere, giving an appearance of wilderness. The road leading to it was badly lit.

The taxi halted a hundred yards before reaching it. The road took a turn here, and once you turned, the bungalow could be seen. Leaving one of the drivers as a guard, the others all walked silently down the road towards the guest house.

On turning the corner, they halted. They saw that a private car was standing in front of the bungalow. There was a light on inside one of the rooms. Obviously, the culprit was preparing to abscond in the night itself. He had to be stopped at all cost.

There was a hurried consultation between all of them.

'Remember, he has a gun and will not hesitate to use it,' warned Sunny.

'Don't worry, I'll manage him,' said Shah Nawaz Khan cockily.

After that, all of them separated.

Chapter 35

The taxi carrying the two old ladies came to a halt in front of the police *chowki*, or police station, in the city. The two ladies got down and accompanied by the driver entered it, to find no one on duty outside. Loud noise could be heard coming from inside the *chowki*. They followed the sound and on entering the one-room office, found the SHO and the constable, who should have been outside, watching a movie on TV while drinking tea. Their uniform was in disarray, and they lay sprawling in their chairs. The sound of the TV was so high that neither of them was aware that anyone had entered the room.

'Good evening. We want to register a complaint,' said Mrs. Rai politely.

There was no response from the two men in uniform, who were obviously enjoying the movie and could not hear anything.

'Good evening! We want to register a complaint. We need your help,' said Mrs. Bhandari more loudly.

Still there was no response from the men watching the TV. In exasperation, their taxi driver suddenly strode forward and picking up the remote, which was lying upon the table, switched off the TV.

'What the hell . . . !' exclaimed the SHO, suddenly becoming aware of the three people who had entered his room. He turned and glared at them, while the other policeman scrambled up and also stood glaring at the trio.

'Who are you, and what are you doing in my room without my permission?' demanded the SHO belligerently.

'Yes. Whom did you ask? This is saheb's room!' said the other man.

'Ask permission? Ask permission from whom? There was no one outside,' said Mrs. Rai.

'We did ask when we came in but you were so busy seeing the movie . . .' began Mrs. Bhandari but the SHO glared at her.

'Shut up and get out. You cannot just walk in here as if it was your home.'

Mrs. Rai looked grimly at him. 'Look here, young man. We have come here to register a complaint and get help. Is it our fault that there was no one there to give us permission to enter?'

At last, very grudgingly, the SHO asked the three of them to sit and tell their story. Two very excited old ladies told him their story. All the while, the SHO looked at them through narrowed eyes and it was obvious that he did not believe them.

'This seems to be rather a tall tale. Are you both sure it is true? I just cannot go around arresting perfectly respectable people on just your say so. You must file a proper written complaint through proper channels and then we will take action,' he said.

'But by then, the scoundrel will have escaped,' said the taxi driver in despair.

The SHO glared at him. 'Take these mad old women from my office. Otherwise, I'll put you in jail.'

The taxi driver realised that the SHO was not going to do anything. So he said softly to the two old ladies, '*Maa ji*, let us go.'

'But . . .' began Mrs. Bhandari but Mrs. Rai caught hold of her hand and dragged her friend out with her. As they left the office, they heard the SHO muttering, '*Pagal log. Bhagwan jaane kaahaan kaahaan se chaley aatey hain*,' (Mad people. God knows from where all they come.) and then the TV was switched on once again.

The two old ladies and the taxi driver went back to his taxi and sat in it.

'What do we do now?' wondered Mrs. Bhandari.

'Wait a minute. Let me phone up Surendra, my nephew. Maybe he can help,' said Mrs. Rai.

A few minutes later, she was talking to a very astonished Surendra. When he heard about all that had happened and how the police had refused to register a complaint, he said, 'Wait a minute, Bua. I know the Deputy Commissioner of Police. He has an account in my bank. I'll just ring him up.'

The result was that very soon, an astonished SHO got a call from the Deputy Commissioner of Police himself. On hearing who was at the other end of the line, the man sprang to attention and sweat broke out on his forehead.

'Yes, sir! Yes, sir! I did not know, sir! Definitely, sir. Yes. Immediate action will be taken.'

Five minutes later, the very man who had so unceremoniously thrown the two old ladies out of his room half an hour earlier escorted them in himself and even offered them tea, listened once again to their story, and immediately called for his jeep and another one and some more constables to go to the guest house to apprehend the villainous professor.

'But what about registering the complaint properly?' asked Mrs. Rai.

'That can be done later, *maa ji*. We must catch the culprit before he escapes. You never told me you knew the Deputy Commissioner saheb himself, *maa ji*!' he said most reproachfully. Mrs. Rai smiled at him and patted his hand. 'It is all right. Let us go. We don't want that villain to escape, do we!'

Chapter 36

At the guest house, Bholu waited impatiently in the private car for Dr. Dastoor to come out from the guest house. He was the driver of the private car. It had been an exciting evening for him, and he smiled at the shock he had seen upon the faces of the three prisoners. He wished Dr. Dastoor had not been in such a tearing hurry to get back to Delhi. He would have loved to torture the prisoners a little. It would have been good sport. He would have wanted to also celebrate with a drink or two, but all Dr. Dastoor had offered him was a bottle of water. The man was a miser alright. The only thing was that since he had drunk all the water, now his bladder was full. He decided to answer the call of nature and went towards some bushes. He had just finished his business and was just zipping himself up when something hit him on the head and he just collapsed and knew no more. When he came to, he found himself trussed up like a turkey, gagged with his own *gamccha*, and lying behind some bushes. He tried to roll over, but he found that he had been stripped of his outer clothes and tied to a tree and could just barely turn over. He looked around and could see the guest house and saw that now someone else had taken his place in the car. The man was wearing Bholu's clothes and, in the dim light, could be mistaken for Bholu himself.

Bholu struggled to free himself and tried to shout, but the gag stuffed in his mouth nearly choked him. He wondered who had hit him and what exactly was happening. The light in the guest room occupied by Dr. Dastoor was switched off. Bholu saw him come out onto the veranda carrying his laptop and holding onto the box they had taken from the three young people inside the premises of the fort. He also had a carpet bag upon his shoulder. He quickly came down from the veranda and, opening the backdoor of the car, got in. He said something to the driver, who nodded. The car started off. As it emerged from the gate of the guest house, after a few moments, the taxi that had been parked near the wall in the shadows started following it.

Inside the car, Dr. Dastoor clutched the precious box with both hands and relaxed. He had told the man he thought was Bholu to rush to the railway station as he wanted to catch the train to Delhi that went past at ten o'clock.

The car reached a deserted stretch of road and halted abruptly.

'What's the matter, Bholu?' asked Dr. Dastoor impatiently.

Shah Nawaz Khan, who had replaced Bholu, muttered something under his breath and got out of the car and opened the bonnet to investigate. The first thing he did was unscrew something and quietly pocket it. The taxi had stopped just out of sight around a bend, and the others were watching tensely. Radhika had crept away and contacted her grandmother on a phone she had borrowed from Shah Nawaz Khan.

'Daadi Maa, where are you? Is the police coming? The crook is already trying to run away. Our friend Shah

Nawaz Khan is trying his level best to delay him, but I have no idea for how long he will be able to do it.'

Daadi Maa's phone was answered by a male voice. 'This is the SHO of the fort circle speaking. Where are you all? Give your location. We'll be there.'

Radhika quickly shared their location over her mobile. The SHO confirmed that he had received their location.

Meanwhile, Dr. Dastoor was getting impatient. He poked his head out of the window and called out to the man bent inside the bonnet.

'What's the matter? At this rate, I'll miss the train, Bholu.'

Khan muttered something under his breath. But Dr. Dastoor suddenly felt suspicious. He left the box inside the car and, getting out, approached the man. Half a moon had come up by now, and its silver rays glinted upon metal. The group watching was horrified. Dr. Dastoor was holding a gun.

Khan suddenly felt cold metal against his neck.

'You are not Bholu! Who are you, and what are you doing here?' asked Dr. Dastoor in a cold voice.

Khan stood back from the open bonnet of the car and put up his hands.

'There is nothing wrong with the car, is there?' asked Dr. Dastoor.

Khan did not bother to reply.

'Close the bonnet and step back. Where is Bholu?' asked Dr. Dastoor menacingly. 'And don't try anything smart.

This gun is loaded, and I will not hesitate to blow your head off.'

Khan laughed in his face. 'I am a friend of the people you stole that box from. You'll never get away with it,' he said triumphantly.

Dr. Dastoor's face flushed with anger. Next moment, he had hit Khan savagely on the side of his face with his gun, making him gasp and collapse to the ground and drawing blood.

The group around the corner watched in horror. 'Shall we rush him?' asked Sunny.

'He is too far off. Immediately he realises the game is up, that villain will shoot Khan bhai,' whispered one of the other two drivers who had accompanied them.

Near the stranded car, Dr. Dastoor hit Khan with the gun once more. 'Get the bloody thing started,' he growled.

'I can't,' said Khan triumphantly, even as he winced with pain.

'What do you mean by that?' demanded Dr. Dastoor.

'Well, a nut seems to have fallen off and the engine won't start,' he said.

'How could a nut have fallen off?' demanded a desperate Dr. Dastoor.

'Well . . . these are old cars,' said Khan, trying to wipe the blood dripping from his cheek with an old rag he had produced from his pocket. 'I am afraid you will have to walk to the station.'

Dr. Dastoor looked furious. Then he caught hold of Khan by his collar and hauling him up, pushed him towards the back of the car. He shoved open the door and told him to pick up his bag and the little box.

'I have to walk. But don't think I am letting you go. You go with me as a hostage,' said Dr. Dastoor.

Khan had no choice. He had to pick up the little carpet bag and the *paan-daan* and then, with Dr. Dastoor walking behind him with the gun trained upon him, the two of them started off.

The watching group had a hurried consultation and decided to follow on foot as following in the taxi would expose them. And they were not sure how long the police would take to reach. If before the police reached they managed to reach a place where another taxi was available, then the culprit might yet escape.

The little group had hardly gone a hundred yards when they heard the sound of a vehicle coming down the road. Even as they looked in the feeble light shed by the moon, a small car came down the road. Dr. Dastoor pushed Khan in the middle of the road and asked him to hail the driver. Khan had no choice. He stood in the middle of the road trying to signal with one hand while clutching the *paan-daan* in the other. The headlights of the car fell upon his bloodied face, and it came to an abrupt halt. A burly Sikh stuck his head out from the driver's window and asked, 'I say, what has happened? Has there been an accident?'

Before Khan could say a word, he was pushed aside and the startled driver found himself looking down the barrel of a revolver.

'Get out. I want your car,' said Dr. Dastoor abruptly. 'You put my bag and the box in the back seat,' he said to Khan, hitting him again unnecessarily. 'Otherwise, I shoot this man.'

By now, the group following on foot was very near. They could see and hear everything and Khan's friends saw red. After that, what followed was more like a comedy sequence in a movie. As the startled driver of the car opened his door to get out, Khan opened the back door. Simultaneously, one of Khan's friends launched himself at Dr. Dastoor from behind and the man fell hard inside the open backdoor of the car. His gun went off with a bang. By now, Sunny and the others had also come up. Just then, there was a sound of two vehicles coming up and round the corner came two police jeeps full of constables led by the SHO and with the two old grannies with them. They came to a halt next to the car where Dr. Dastoor was struggling for all he was worth, but as he tried to hold on to the gun and fire it, suddenly one skinny old arm snaked in through the other window and catching hold of his wrist, twisted it smartly, making him howl. Even as the gun dropped from his hand, it was snatched away. It was the senior Mrs. Rai, who had sneaked up from the other side. By now, the police had encircled the car and very soon, a very angry looking Dr. Dastoor stood handcuffed and cursing on the side of the road while two very excited groups of people talked to each other, exchanging notes.

The SHO soon called for attention and said they had to go to the police station so a report could be filed.

Some time later, they all were sitting in the police station when suddenly Dr. Dastoor seemed to come to a decision of some sort. He turned and addressed the SHO, who was busy writing a report for the Commissioner of Police.

Radhika had grabbed the *paan-daan* and was holding onto it.

'That box belongs to me, SHO saheb. These people are trying to steal it from me!' declared Dr. Dastoor venomously.

Radhika, Shalini, Sunny and the two old ladies froze. Khan and his friend were sitting outside the room as there was not enough room for them inside it.

'I found it hidden in the fort while I was exploring it. I was taking it to get it registered at the Archaeological Survey of India,' declared Dr. Dastoor.

'If it belongs to you, tell me what it contains?' challenged Radhika.

'Well, I never managed to open it, so I don't know,' said Dr. Dastoor defensively.

'But I know,' said Radhika triumphantly. 'It has a letter in English by Rani Laxmi Bai, a few wooden toys belonging to her adopted son, along with a quill with her name engraved in gold upon it.'

'Yes, SHO saheb. In fact, Radhika found a map showing where the late yuvraj had buried it. She wanted to show it to me and get it authenticated when this villain here stole it from us and locked us all inside that old passage that leads from the palace to the *pilkhana*. He intended for us to die there as most people have forgotten about that old passage and he was not going to tell anyone about where we were. If these dear old ladies had not found us, we would still be there,' declared Shalini.

'He apprehended you all all alone?' asked the SHO, looking at them.

'Oh my God! We forgot about Bholu!' exclaimed Sunny.

'Bholu? Who is he?' asked the SHO with interest.

Radhika explained who Bholu was and what they had done with him.

'He must be still there, tied to that tree,' said Sunny, getting up.

'Where are you going?' demanded the SHO.

'To get Bholu,' said Sunny.

'Sit down, young man. I'll send two men to get him.'

The SHO was as good as his word. Half an hour later, while the entire party in the SHO's office except for Dr. Dastoor was sipping hot tea, a very sorry looking Bholu was pushed into the room. Very soon, they were joined by Surendra, who had come in his car. The best was when suddenly the Commissioner of Police himself landed up. There was such a hullabaloo and so much excitement! It was nearly morning before Dr. Dastoor, all the time belligerently demanding that he wanted a lawyer, and Bholu were booked and locked up in jail and the others were allowed to go back home. The two old ladies thanked the Commissioner of Police, who gallantly told them, '*Maa ji*, after all, we in the police force are always there to help you, especially the family of any of our brothers in the armed forces. They keep us safe, and we keep their families safe,' he declared.

Chapter 37

It was a week later. The Rai family was having breakfast. Brigadier Rai had returned with his wife and son for a few days of casual leave to Noida and, as usual, was buried in his newspaper. Suddenly, he came across a startling piece of news. Apparently, a Ms. Radhika Rai had found an old map showing where the late yuvraj of Jhansi had buried something. Ms. Radhika Rai had approached her friend Dr. Shalini Mehta, who was in charge of the restoration going on in the fort and palace at Jhansi, and the two of them, with the help of another friend, Mr. Sunny Bhandari, had dug up the treasure, which had turned out to be an old brass *paan-daan*. On opening the *paan-daan*, they had found that it contained some wooden toys and a personal quill engraved in gold belonging to Rani Laxmi Bai. The most important thing was that there was a letter written in English, signed by the rani, with her stamp upon it, proving beyond doubt that the rani knew English.

Brigadier Rai looked up from his paper at his daughter, who was busy eating her breakfast. 'Is this news about you, Radhika?' he asked, waving the paper at her.

'What news?' asked Radhika.

'This about finding some buried *paan-daan*. And who is this Dr. Shalini Mehta? How do you know her?'

'Oh Papa, she is Shalini *didi*. Remember your first CO and later your brigade commander, Brigadier Mehta? His daughter.'

'Oh. And how did you meet her? How is she and how are her parents?' asked Brigadier Rai, brightening up.

For a moment, there was silence around the dining table. Then, Radhika swallowed hard and told a truncated version of all that had happened. The only thing she glossed over was how she found the location of the treasure. She said she had discovered the map giving the location of the buried *paan-daan* by chance inside a book in the library of Jhansi fort, where she had gone just to read up about the rani a little more. There, she had discovered Dr. Mehta, who was in charge of the restoration and had given a lecture at Delhi University just a few months back. Before Radhika could continue with the rest of the adventure, Daadi Maa interrupted and smoothly changed the topic.

Brigadier Rai went back to his paper.

Radhika looked at her Daadi Maa, who winked at her. It was obvious she did not want her son to know the full details of the story, especially not about the time travel in the lift or about the kidnapping and how they all had outwitted the villain Dr. Dastoor.

There was another short paragraph on the fourth page about a Dr. Dastoor, the head of the Department of History at Delhi University, who had been accused of going on archaeological digs, stealing archaeological finds of other people and passing them off as his own, and even attempting to murder people. The court had barred him from going on any archaeological dig ever, fined him a hefty sum, and given him a jail term of ten years. There was no mention of any magic lift, time travel, etc.

GLOSSARY

adda: a hideout

agarbatti: an incense stick

angan: a courtyard

angithi: a traditional brazier usually made of mud and stone and used for cooking

anna: a currency unit formerly used in British India, equal to 1/16 of a rupee

antakshari: a game in which a team sings a song and the next team must sing a song beginning with the letter the first team's song ended with

akhara: a traditional Indian arena for wrestling and other physical forms of exercise, usually with a dirt floor

ayah: a caretaker

badam: almond

badshah: an emperor

bahu: a daughter-in-law

baithak: a withdrawing room

bandobast: arrangements

bania: a shopkeeper

baraat: the celebratory wedding procession that accompanies a groom

beedis: local cigarettes made from tobacco wrapped in dried tendu leaves tied with a string *beta*: a reference to a son or a generic reference to any child

bhaiya: a reference to a brother

bhajan: a hymn; a religious song of praise

bhaji: diced, lightly spiced vegetables cooked in a little oil or ghee

bhature: fluffy deep-fried bread made from leavened sourdough

Brahmin: a member of the highest Hindu caste

buddy: the personal assistant, usually a soldier from a lower rank, the army provides to each officer

chai: tea

chana-jor-garam: a savoury, crunchy snack made from cooked black gram that has been flattened, fried, and seasoned with spices

changu: a sidekick

chapatti: a round flat unleavened bread of India that is usually made of whole-wheat flour and cooked on a griddle

chaukidar: a watchman

chhole: a spicy chickpea preparation

choli: a blouse

Daadi: a reference to a paternal grandmother

Daada: a reference to a paternal grandfather

daal: lentil

darshan: a visit to a sacred shrine to view an image or idol of the deity and offer prayers

devi: a goddess

dharam: the things a person must do as a religious and moral duty

dhaba: a road-side food stall

dhoti: a length of material tied around the loins, usually covering the entire legs

didi: a reference to a sister

dupatta: a length of material worn around the neck and shoulders, typically with a *salwar kameez*

gamchha: a scarf of sorts normally made of cotton

gunda: a goon

fauj: the army

fauji: a member of the armed forces

firangi: foreign

guru: a teacher

haathi-khana: where elephants are kept

halwai: a confectioner, one who makes traditional Indian sweets

haveli: a mansion

howdah: The seat on top of an elephant in which people sit

kadahi: a type of wok

Kunwar: an Indian title denoting a prince

kurta: a loose, collarless tunic worn by people in South Asia, usually over a *pyjama* or any other ethnic lower

paan: betel leaf

pakore: fritters made from potato or vegetable wedges coated in seasoned gram flour batter and deep fried

papad: dough made of bean, rice, or lentil flour rolled out into wafer-thin rounds and either deep fried or dry heated over an open flame

paranthe: a layered, usually whole-wheat flatbread, made with ghee or oil, and often stuffed with lentils, potatoes, or other vegetables

martaban: a large glazed pottery jar usually meant for storing pickles, preserves, etc.

murukku: a savoury crunchy snack in the form of a pinwheel, made from rice flour, and gram (chickpea) flour, spiced with onion, cumin, and chili

laddoo: a spherical sweet from the Indian Subcontinent made of various ingredients and sugar syrup or jaggery

lassi: a traditional drink made with curd, water, sugar, and cardamom or saffron

lehenga: a traditional full ankle-length skirt worn by Indian women, usually on formal or ceremonial occasions

lota: a small round waterpot, usually of bronze

maa ji: a respectful reference to one's mother

mahaut: the caretaker of an elephant

malkhamb: a form of ancient martial art originating in the Indian Subcontinent *mandir*: a temple, for worship

mausi: a reference to a maternal aunt

mohar: a sovereign or a coin

namakpare: a kind of dry savoury snack made of flour dough that is deep fried

nari sena: an army made up of women

nauvari: a nine-yard *saree*

nazarana: a gift

paan-daan: a box to keep betelnuts and betel leaves in

pagal gymkhana: an afternoon of fun and games held by a unit of the defence forces for soldiers and their families

pahar: a traditional unit of time used in the Indian Subcontinent, equal to an eighth of a day, that is, three hours

palki: a palanquin

pallav: the end of a *saree* that usually goes over one shoulder and hangs free

pilkhana: where elephants are kept

poori: unleavened flat bread rolled out into thin circles and deep fried

purdah: a practice where women remain secluded from public observation by wearing veils or always remaining behind high-walled enclosures, curtains, etc.

raita: a savoury curd preparation

rani: a queen

roti: another name for a *chapatti*

sadhu: a Hindu holy man who has chosen to live apart from society

saheli: a reference to a friend

samosa: a small triangular pastry case containing spiced vegetables or meat and served fried

sandook: a box

sarkar: government; also a term of respect for someone

sardar: the leader of a group or a village

saree: a garment consisting of a length of cotton or silk elaborately draped around the body, traditionally worn by women from South Asia

shakarpare: a kind of sweet made of flour dough deep fried, dipped in sugar syrup, and further cooked till dry

sharbat: a cold drink

tekri: a knoll

teli: a caste traditionally in the business of oil pressing and trade in India, Nepal, and Pakistan

thali: a plate or a round platter used to serve food in South Asia

utthak baithak: a form of squats

yuvraj: a prince who is the next in line to be the king; the heir apparent

Author's Note

The idea for writing a story about time travel in a magic lift came from the fact that recently, my daughters got a lift put for my use in our flat, which happens to be on the top floor in a sector in Noida where there are no lifts and the population consists of ageing retirees, 60% of who reside on the first, second, or third floor. A lot of the aged population was beginning to despair and selling their beloved flats and going away as they thought that the authorities would not allow any lifts to be put. This lift became a sort of nine-day wonder, a magical thing that put heart and hope in people who had given up literally. People suddenly realised that they could get a lift put officially, with the blessing of the Noida Authorities, and did not have to sell off their flats if they could not climb the stairs as they grew old. Not only did a huge wave of hope flood the ageing community in Noida, but its effect was felt as far off as Greater Noida, Pitampura, and Gurugram. People have been coming to see the lift and find out the procedure of how to go about getting one installed in their own group of flats. Already, many lifts have been put and the wave of hope that has engulfed the retired community is unbelievable. The lift seems to have developed magical powers of attraction and exudes hope, thus leading to this idea of a magic lift.

The secret tunnel in which the lift landed up and which led to the room of the yuvraj is a figment of my imagination. But most palaces do have secret tunnels that lead from the chief chambers to outside the fort or city so that if there was a crisis, the rulers and their families could escape. Jhansi Fort is also known to have had one that led from one corner to beyond the town and came out there.

The story of Jokhan Bagh is true and so is the help the rani sent in the form of food through her *sahelis* to the starving British hiding inside Star Fort. She refused to fight a starving enemy, nor did she believe in waging war upon women and children.

I decided that my heroin will go back to 1857–58 as right from childhood, I have been fascinated by the story of Rani Laxmi Bai. As a child, I remember pretending to be her and brandishing an imaginary sword while riding an imaginary horse, yelling at the top of my lungs for the British to quit Bharat, not realising that the British had already left Bharat. I wanted to grow up to be like Rani Laxmi Bai, wanting to learn riding, shooting, archery, wrestling, etc. At one stage, I even contemplated joining Vanasthali Vidya Peeth, a school where I was told all these sports were taught to girls.

Most of the incidents described in this book in connection with Rani Laxmi Bai actually took place.

The story of Jhalkari bai is a recorded fact. She bore a striking resemblance to the rani. Born in 1830 in Bhoja village, she belonged to the Dalit Kori caste. She learnt how to use weapons early in life, and there are tales of her bravery when she fought a tiger single handed with just a stick and when she chased away some dacoits who had come to rob her village. She learnt archery, shooting, and wrestling from her husband Puran Kori, who was a soldier in the army of Raja Gangadhar Rao, the husband of Rani Laxmi Bai, and later served in the rani's own army.

Jhalkari bai joined the rani's Durga Dal, her *nari sena* or women brigade, as an ordinary foot soldier but because of her extraordinary abilities soon rose to a position of leadership and trust. Many times, she took advantage of her resemblance to the rani and replaced her in battle. When the rani had to flee Jhansi in the night, having been betrayed by one of her own *sardars*, Jhalkari bai, to allow the rani time to get away, impersonated her and rode out to the British camp and dared them to arrest her. The British were fooled for a few hours and had to call in someone who knew the rani. Only then was it discovered that it was not the rani who had surrendered but Jhalkari bai. It is not very clear whether they released her or hanged her. Some say she died many years later of old age. She still lives on in the folklore of Bundelkhand, and many Dalit communities of the area revere her as a *devi* and even celebrate Jhalkari Jayanti every year in her honour.

The story of how the rani and her friend lifted off the rebel Sagar Singh from a running horse is true. So is the story of him having joined her army. He later on gave a good account of himself during battle and fought bravely for her against the British, laying down his life for her.

The story of the betrayal by Rao Dulhaju is also true. If he had not betrayed the rani and opened the gates of Jhansi, Jhansi would not have fallen for many more days.

There was a contingent of Pathans in the rani's army. When they joined her, they had been in a miserable condition. The rani gave them not only shelter but also good weapons and good pay and they were ever grateful to her and gave a very good account of themselves in her service. Their leader was one Gul Mohammad, who pledged his life to the rani and her cause.

There is a controversy about the rani knowing English. It is believed that she spoke broken English but whether she could write it or not is not very clear.

The only likeness or photograph of the rani was taken in 1850, when she was 22 years old, by a British photographer masquerading as a German named Hoffman. If the rani had known the man was British, she would never have agreed and allowed him to take a likeness of her. But this again is not authenticated.

Very few people know that Damodar Rao, the yuvraj of Jhansi, grew up to become a good photographer and a good artist.

This book has been written as light reading for the young adult. I have tried to keep to the known historical facts as much as possible. Any mistakes or inaccuracies are all my own.

About the Author

Savita Singh

Savita Singh has been writing professionally since 1979 and has written more than 300 published short stories, articles, poems, dramas, etc, including twenty-two books. She writes in English and Hindi and has written right from children's literature, to Mills & Boon kind of romances, to human-interest stories and some T.V. serials. She has done translation work from Hindi to English as well as a stint as agony aunt.

In 2024, at the Kolkata Book Fest, she was presented the Fiction Book of the Year award for her book *Dwarka* by Ukiyoto. The award was sponsored by the Ministry of Tourism, Govt. of India.

She was married to an army officer who died in a tragic helicopter accident in Rajouri, J&K, while on duty in 1990. She has been published in magazines like *Woman's Era*, *Champak*, *Femina*, *Sainik Samachar*, and *Illustrated Weekly*. Her books have been published by India Book House, Rupa, Strategic Books, Ukiyoto, etc.

www.ingramcontent.com/pod-product-compliance
Lightning Source LLC
LaVergne TN
LVHW041702070526
838199LV00045B/1163